GAMEWORLD

"Want a thrill? Ride a longboard down a waterslide or plunge into *Game World*. The rush will be the same."
—Colin Channer, author of *The Girl with the Golden Shoes*

GAMEWORLD

C.J. FARLEY

A NOVEL

Published by Akashic Books
Text ©2014 C.J. Farley
Illustrations ©2014 Yongjin Im

Hardcover ISBN-13: 978-1-61775-305-3
Paperback ISBN-13: 978-1-61775-197-4

Library of Congress Control Number: 2013938805

First printing

Black Sheep
c/o Akashic Books
PO Box 1456
New York, NY 10009
info@akashicbooks.com
www.akashicbooks.com

More books for young readers from Black Sheep:

Changers Book One: Drew
by T Cooper and Allison Glock-Cooper

Pills & Starships
by Lydia Millet
(forthcoming)

BOOK ONE

THE GAME CHANGERS

Check out the Xamaicapedia *excerpt at the end of the book for a glossary of terms.*

CHAPTER ONE

"Are you a Game Changer?"

At 8:23 a.m., Dylan spied Emma coming up to him at his locker. He looked around but there was no place to hide. Winston Macintosh Middle School was filled with yawning kids trudging grudgingly down the grungy hallways to their boring morning classes. Emma was Dylan's little sister, but she wasn't so little—she was almost the same height as him, and he was one of the tallest kids in sixth grade. She was also really smart, so even though she was three years younger, she had skipped up to Dylan's grade, and he found this so embarrassing he tried never to be spotted with her on school grounds. But now here she was, standing right next to him for all his friends to see. Not that he had that many friends.

Dylan tied back his dreadlocks and tried to act cool. "What do you want?"

As usual, Dylan and Emma were dressed like they were from two different families, maybe even different planets. Dylan was wearing ripped black jeans, skater sneakers he had bought used online, and a T-shirt with the name of a band that had broken up before he was even born. Emma had on a school uniform—blue blazer, white knee socks, and a black skirt—which was weirder than you might think because Winston Macintosh was a public school that didn't have uniforms. They barely had classrooms.

Emma leaned in so close her braids brushed Dylan's ears. "Are you a Game Changer?"

"Why are you asking?"

"Chad Worthington is telling people that if you are, he's gonna beat the snot out of you."

"You think I don't know that?" Dylan replied, although he did not, in fact, know that.

"He told Anjali he's gonna turn you upside down and mop the cafeteria with your dreads."

"So?"

"You're not scared or anything? Want me to walk with you to language arts?"

"Like I want to be seen in public with Viral Emma. No offense."

"Whatever," Emma shrugged. "Just remember what the philosopher Sun Tzu said . . ."

Dylan knew what was coming and covered his ears. "Not listening! La-la-la-la!"

"Winning without fighting is the ultimate martial art," she quoted anyway.

Dylan, his fingers still in his ears, rushed away from his sister as fast as he could—and nearly slammed right into Ivan, a spiky-haired seventh grader so big he looked like he had swallowed a couple sixth graders.

The hulking kid pretended to throw a punch and when Dylan jerked back to dodge it, Ivan laughed. "You're no Game Changer! For real, though, at three p.m. the Chadster is gonna end you! Sucks to be you right now, don't it, Loopy?"

Ivan, who was chewing a wad of gum the size of a hamster, popped a bubble, faked another punch at Dylan's head, and lumbered away.

Dylan was officially freaking out. He often felt like he had sixteen browser windows open in his head all at once. Now it felt like he had 160. Why did Chad think he was a Game Changer? Was this a Loopy thing? He and Emma were both in the accelerated group at school—technically it was named the Learning Outlier Opportunity Program, but in reality everyone called them Loopys. Other kids, even members of the glee club, were constantly tripping Loopys in the hall, knocking lunch trays out of their hands, or locking them in their own lockers.

Maybe there was something to Emma's warning. But Dylan barely even knew Chad, a sofa-sized seventh grader who hung out with gum-chewing goons like Ivan. And after the whole Viral Emma thing, Dylan tried to steer completely clear of Chad and his crew, who were the kind of jerks who spent the school day in the parking lot, bullying scrawny kids, torturing small mammals, and seeing who could fart the loudest. If passing gas ever became an Olympic sport, Chad and his goons would be gold medalists. So why were Chad and his butt-trumpet bunch gunning for Dylan?

At 12:05 p.m., Dylan reported to language arts in the Loopy wing, a cluster of rooms tucked away in the school's leaky basement, which, depending on the day, smelled like old roadkill, wet sneakers, or public transportation. As Dylan walked into room 103, up on the blackboard, scrawled in red chalk, he saw this message:

GAME OVER LOOPY.
I'M COMIN FOR YOU AT 3.
THE CHADSTER

The language arts teacher didn't even do anything about the threat until halfway through the period—and then she didn't erase it, she just added a "g" to the end of "comin." As Dylan scurried out of the room, trying to figure out how he could escape Chad and his goons, Eli Marquez, another sixth grade Loopy, rolled up in his wheelchair.

"*Hola!* I've got some intel on Chad," Eli announced, whipping out his computer and peering at the screen through his glasses, which magnified his sea-green eyes to a cartoon size. He had a shock of straight black hair he never combed except with his fingers, and he carried around this plaid thingy he called a *snuglet* that was a cross between a sweater and a blanket and guaranteed nobody but Dylan would ever sit with him during lunch.

"How did you get info on Chad?" Dylan asked.

"Dude, how long have we known each other?" Eli replied.

"Don't tell me you hacked into Chad's computer."

"Then I won't tell you that. 'Cause I hacked his phone."

Dylan bumped fists with Eli. "Sweet! So why does Chad want to murder me?"

"Because he thinks you're a Game Changer—and he's afraid he's not."

"Seriously? This is really about a video game?"

Everyone at the school was into a video game called Xamaica, and there was a huge tournament coming up. Only the forty-four best players got to enter—the *Game Changers*, they called them. So the question running through the halls was, *Are you a Game Changer?* Nobody knew the answer—yet.

"They're gonna announce who made the Game Changers tonight," Eli explained. "Chad wants to kill you before that happens."

"That's insane! I couldn't afford a ticket even if I was picked!"

"Xamaica is a stupid game from an idiotic company, but you're a beast at it. And if you're awesome at something, morons like Chad try to eat you alive. You know the way zombies are stupid but they always devour people's brains? It's the same principle."

Dylan felt his forehead get hot. There was a secret to why he was so great at Xamaica—it was something he hadn't even told Eli and that he could never let Chad find out. "This is a nightmare."

"It gets worse. If he catches you, he's gonna give you the gas."

This was bad. Chad had a habit of sitting on his enemies and farting on them. Once he did that you were basically so humiliated you had to change schools. "What's my move?"

Eli smiled. "Well, I have a plan."

Dylan frowned. "I was afraid you'd say that."

Thirteen minutes until the Chad Attack. Whenever goons came after Eli, he would say his asthma was acting up and get a pass to leave school. At 2:47 p.m., taking Eli's advice, Dylan went to the nurse's office, a small windowless room that seemed purposely designed to be no fun at all.

Ms. Barett, the school nurse, was a tiny woman with small eyes that darted around her face like scared mice. "What are you here for?" she asked.

"I'm not feeling well," Dylan wheezed. "Can I get a note to go home early?"

The nurse looked skeptical. "You seem fine."

"But you know I have—that condition. It's acting up again."

"Your attention problems?"

"You know I take stuff for that."

"Your insomnia?"

"That's because of the stuff I take."

"The bouts of rage? The nail-biting?"

"I'm trying, okay? Anyway, I mean the other-other-other thing."

The nurse flipped through a manila folder stuffed with Dylan's medical records. "I see from last time that you got those nasty scratches on your chest when you were playing a video game. Are you having another episode?"

"Yeah, I guess kinda," he sorta lied.

"Hmmm. I can't read this chicken scratch for your emergency contact—should I call your mother . . . father . . . other?"

"I tell you this every time! I don't really have a family. I live with the Professor . . . I mean my aunt. She's definitely more of an other than a mother."

The nurse picked up the phone. "Well, we can contact her."

"Do you have to get her involved? Can't you just write me a note?"

She put down the phone. "This wouldn't be about Chad Worthington, would it?"

Dylan nearly fell off the white stool he was sitting on. "Why does everyone know about this?"

"Chad is the new school superintendant's son. News travels. He's gotten into lots of fights—even with his buddies. Whatever you do, don't let him give you the gas."

"You know about that? You have to help me!"

The nurse's rodent eyes stopped scampering, like they had been caught in a trap.

"I can give you a head start," she said.

Nurse Barett let him go to his locker and get his stuff, but it was already 2:55 p.m. and classes were letting out in just five minutes. Dylan ran at full speed down the empty hallway. As he passed the gym, he saw some of Chad's thugs pressing their faces against the windows of the double doors, chewing on wads of gum and pointing menacingly at him. Dylan reached his locker with two minutes to spare—and then the bell rang early. Did nothing in this crummy school work right? Kids spilled into the hall—Chad would be somewhere in the spillage. Dylan looked around. Maybe in all the confusion he could slip out the east wing side doors, near the science labs. Then it would be a straight shot to Webster Avenue and freedom.

"Dylan! I'm coming for you, Loopy!"

Too late. Chad burst out of Spanish class like a bull charging a matador. Dylan got a quick glimpse: his bonfire of red hair, his freckled face, his left cheek eternally bulging with a glob of gum. He had a little crimson fuzz on his lip, and word was that he sometimes even shaved his chin. As Chad passed, the crowds in the hall parted like a zipper unzipping, letting him roar by. Three of his crew, blowing bubbles as they ran, were right behind him.

"Game over, Loopy!" Chad bellowed. "That's right, I said it!"

No way could Dylan outrun this jerk. But maybe there was another way.

He grabbed his skateboard out of his locker. He didn't have the cash for a new board, so over the last few months he had built this himself from secondhand parts. He hoped all the work paid off now.

Dylan skated down the hall, weaving around students. A couple goons tried to grab him, but he slid right by them. The main door to the school was coming up, and Chad was closing fast, only two classrooms away. "I have you now!" he yowled.

"Fight! Fight! Fight!" the students all around started chanting.

"Get ready for the gas!" Chad reached out and managed to get a paw on Dylan's ankle. Just then, Dylan heard a sound like a trumpet crossed with an elephant and something streaked out of nowhere and crashed into Chad's legs. Dylan stumbled off his skateboard and kept running out the school's front door; Chad lost his footing and went crashing to the floor along with whatever it was that had taken him out.

Eli had tripped up Chad. Anjali—who was also a Loopy but was weirder than most because she was always lugging around a French horn—had helped out by pushing Eli and his chair right in front of Dylan's pursuer.

Chad, getting to his feet, turned angrily toward the pair, and Dylan kept running, too far ahead now to get caught.

"Keep going!" Eli shouted at Dylan. "What's he gonna do, put me in a wheelchair?"

Should he stay? Should he go? Dylan glanced back over his shoulder at Chad, who was on a rampage, kicking Dylan's abandoned black, gold, and green skateboard, tossing Eli's laptop into a wall, and picking up Anjali's French horn to slam it into the sidewalk. Anjali opened her mouth in a silent scream.

Dylan turned away from the school and kept running up Webster Avenue toward his house, as pea-colored clouds rolled across the late-afternoon sky.

Was he really a Game Changer?

CHAPTER TWO

Dylan was trying to get up the nerve to ask the Professor about Xamaica, and Emma was loving every moment of it. They were all in their cramped apartment sitting at the card table eating a dinner of burnt toast, burnt bacon, and this horrible lemonade made from powder the Professor bought in bulk. One sip tasted worse than sucking on a yellow marker. Two sips were as bad as eating yellow snow. Nobody made it to three.

"Gross!" Dylan grumbled, pushing his half-empty glass to the side. "You know, just because they sell it in bulk doesn't mean we should drink it in bulk."

"Forget that, ask her about the Game Changers!" Emma said.

"Shut up!" Dylan shot back.

At Dylan's outburst, the tiny apartment, which was crammed with birdcages, suddenly came alive with the sounds of all the birds locked in them. The Professor taught avian studies at a small college and she regularly took her work home with her. Unfortunately, her work tended to squawk, chirp, and hoot round the clock.

The Professor sighed. "We talked about this," she said to Dylan in the kind of calming voice that made everyone tense. "You've got to control yourself. You have to grow up."

"Ask her about the thing," Emma prodded Dylan. "You need parental permission."

"Will you stop?" Dylan growled. "She's not my parent and neither are you."

"You don't even remember Mom and Dad," Emma huffed.

"I remember more than you," Dylan countered, even though in truth he only had scattered memories of the accident, like tiny pieces of a puzzle, and not only did he not know how they fit together, some of them were missing.

The Professor, who had been reading *Birdbaths of Ancient Rome: Volume Seven,* slammed the book down on the card table, which nearly buckled under the weight. The glass of lemonade fell to the floor. Dylan and Emma stopped arguing, and even the birds shut up for a moment.

"Let's not argue about your parents," the Professor said. "Your father—my brother—wanted us all to be a family. And I know your mother would have wanted the same thing. She was a mysterious sort; there was something magic about her."

"Why don't you ever tell us stories about them?" Dylan asked.

"The tales can wait," the Professor replied. "What's all this about a game?"

"There's this tournament," Dylan explained. "I want to enter."

"What kind of tournament? Chess?"

"Not exactly. It is a game—a video game."

"A video game tournament?" She said the last three words the way you'd say *Aliens on Mars?* or *Cats speaking Italian?*

Emma, who was at the sink rinsing out the glass Dylan thought he just saw break, interrupted: "It's tonight—tickets are mad expensive."

"Will you shut up?" Dylan said. He turned to the Professor. "I never ask for anything. But I'm good at this game called Xamaica. So that's why I want to go. I just need to borrow . . ."

"Xamaica? I've heard of this game. I know it inspires truancy—and perhaps worse."

"But . . ."

"Enough," the Professor gently commanded, and something about her tone let Dylan know it really was. She took off her horn-rimmed glasses, wiped them on her blouse, and put them back on a little smudgier than they were before. She resembled a bird in many ways: she had a beaklike nose, a spindly cranelike figure, and a voice like a squawk.

"I have some news," the Professor announced after several moments. "And it's time you both heard it."

"What kind of news?" Dylan asked.

"You've both been strong for so many years. Dylan, I know you wear your ripped jeans and T-shirts because you know we can't afford more. And Emma, I appreciate that you wear a uniform because it's less expensive than sporting the latest fashions like the other girls. I'm grateful for your sacrifices. But this tournament is out of the question. We're out of money and out of time. In fact, we have to move."

"What? Why?" Emma and Dylan cried out together.

"My work is controversial and the college eliminated my department to save money."

"What's controversial about birds?" Dylan asked.

"I have been on the hunt for a rare species—the missing link between dinosaurs and birds. My colleagues say it's a myth, that I'm crazy—and now I've been forced out."

Dylan was surprised but not shocked. Social services had paid the apartment more than a few visits, saying that there were too many birds and not enough space. The neighbors were always complaining about the Professor's constant bird-watching because they were totally creeped out when they saw her late at night peering out the window with binoculars. But maybe it was the fact that she wore a bird costume while doing it that made it really seem nuts. Plus, she refused to explain to anyone why she needed heavy rope, tranquilizer darts, and a shark cage to watch birds. It had only been a matter of time before all the weirdness got back to her bosses at the college.

"What I do is for your protection—it's where most of our money goes," the Professor explained. "If I could get proof for my theories . . . I could save my funding . . . our home . . ."

"I don't get it. Why is your research for our protection?" Dylan broke in. "You're always using those binoculars. How many rare birds are you going to spot in downtown New Rock? And seriously, a shark cage? What are you really looking for?"

All the birds in the apartment began to squawk and tweet and rattle their coops.

"I've said all I can say," the Professor concluded. "We have to leave by Friday."

"Where are we going to go?" Emma asked. "What are we going to do for money?"

Then Dylan saw the Professor do something he had never seen her do.

She began to cry.

That night, as usual, Dylan couldn't sleep. Three thousand windows were open in his head. It was bad enough he didn't have a family—now, pretty soon, he wouldn't have a place to live. He flicked on the TV just to get his mind off how his life had become an epic fail.

The Professor hated it when he watched TV because she thought it contributed to his lack of focus. She had stopped paying the cable bill a few months back. Now they only had four channels. Two if it was raining.

All the channels were carrying reports about the Game Changers.

"... *video game Xamaica. Players take on the role of a mythological beast and explore forty-four different levels. Now game-maker Mee Corp. is picking forty-four children for the Tournament of Xamaica* ..."

"... *winner will get what's billed as a Grand Major Triple-Secret Prize. But parents complain the game is already too addictive, and has caused some players to run away from home to spend more time* ..."

"... *sold out all over the city. Analysts worry that Mee Corp. will not be able to keep up with demand* ..."

Dylan stopped on the last channel where there was a commercial for Mee Corp. The head of Ines Mee, the daughter of the company's founder, filled the screen. Her face was as pale and perfectly oval as an egg. She had a shadowy gaze and wore her long dark hair swept over her right eye like a black curtain. She was in all of Mee Corp.'s ads, and the company sold a lot of stuff, everything from potato chips to computer chips. She was only thirteen years old but she had her own reality show—*Mee²*—where she was always having some adventure in some far-off place—partying, skydiving, skiing, partying some more, sarfari-ing (if that's even a word), auto racing, skydiving again, shopping, and it never ended. In each situation she was using some Mee Corp. product.

"*It's gonna be beyond awesome,*" Ines purred. "*So come to the Mee Convention Center tonight—and see if you made the list of Game Changers!*"

Ping!

What was that?

Ping!

Someone had thrown something against the kitchen window. The cockatoos in the kitchenette began to squawk; Dylan gave them crackers to shut them up before they woke up Emma or the Professor. He looked out the window and spotted Eli, one flight below, in his wheelchair on the sidewalk. He was shivering in his snuglet.

"What's up?" Eli called. "I've been throwing rocks for twenty minutes!"

"Ever heard of a doorbell?" Dylan shot back.

"Ever heard of paying your phone bill? Anyway, I didn't want to wake the Prof."

"What's going on? Are you and Anjali okay?"

"We're cool. I can't say the same about Anjali's French horn."

"Why are you here?"

"The Xamaica tournament, man! It's gonna be epic! We gotta go!"

"What do you mean *we*? I thought you hated Xamaica—and Mee Corp.!"

"I still want their prize money, yo! Let's see if our names are on the list!"

Dylan didn't know what to say. He was pretty certain he was one of the best players around, but what if the people who were selecting the top players found out why?

Just then, Dylan heard a bed creak behind him.

Emma was up, clutching the lady pirate doll she always slept with, and she came over to the window. "Don't tell me you're going to the tournament!"

"*Buenas tardes, señorita,*" Eli greeted Emma.

"Hey, Eli," she replied sleepily.

"Eli—why do you always get all *español* around my sister?" Dylan griped. "And Emma—have you not learned your lesson about bringing that doll out in public?"

Emma crossed her arms and looked at Dylan. "What about your condition?"

"His seizures?" Eli asked. "He's a Loopy. We all have issues."

"You didn't tell Eli what triggers them?"

"Shut up!" Dylan snapped. "Didn't you hear the Professor? We might lose the apartment! We need money. If I have a shot at the tournament, I have to take it!"

The cockatoos began to squawk again.

"Then I'm going too," Emma declared.

"Why? Do you think we need you to watch us?" Dylan complained. "Do you think you're smarter than us or something?"

"She *is* smarter than us," Eli pointed out. "Like multiples. She won the state science fair and the state spelling bee."

"Shakespeare once said, *The fool doth think he is wise, but the wise man knows himself to be a fool,*" Emma remarked.

"I have no idea what that means," Dylan said.

"It means she's coming along," Eli laughed. "*Vamanos, muchachos!*"

Every kid in the city was outside the Mee Convention Center in midtown New Rock and there were loads of TV cameras and reporters too. The scene was like a Hollywood movie opening crossed with a football homecoming. Spotlights crisscrossed the air, and a stream of black limos dropped off VIPs. A line of kids, some with tickets, others hoping to score some, snaked around the outside of the building.

"Disgusting," Eli seethed, as he and Emma and Dylan got out of a taxi, and the driver got his wheelchair from the trunk. "Look at all the rich kids cutting the line!"

"I guess they got special invites," Dylan said. "We couldn't afford tickets even if there were any available. How are we going to get in?"

"There's a saying that when one door closes, others open," Emma chimed in.

"And what philosopher said that?" Dylan asked.

"Bob Marley."

"Well, he had it right," Eli winked. "And I have a plan."

Dylan groaned. "Is it better than your science fair plan from last year? We got two weeks detention for that one."

"Totally undeserved," Eli replied. "And not one of those armadillos was hurt."

Eli motioned Dylan and Emma over to the wheelchair entrance; the guard took a look at Eli and waved all three kids inside. "One advantage of being in a wheelchair," Eli confided, as they slipped into the building.

"Are there others?" Dylan asked.

"Well, the chair is a babe magnet," Eli smiled.

Emma pretended the chair's magnetism was drawing her in before laughing.

Dylan, Eli, and Emma wound their way through the corridors until they came to a locked gate. "All the doors here are computer controlled," Eli said. "I got this."

He pulled out his laptop.

"I thought Chad trashed that," Dylan said.

"This computer is waterproof, fireproof, and goon-proof," Eli boasted. "One of my dad's start-up companies designed the case. Problem is, there was a bug."

"A bug? What kind?"

"Lice. Totally infested the factory. So it went bust, like all my dad's start-ups."

Eli typed furiously for a second and then, like a pianist finishing a dramatic solo, hit a single key. The gate slid open and the kids were staring into the stands of an arena. The seats were filled with people, but the floor of the arena was empty except for forty-four spotlights shining on forty-four empty spots. A huge screen was set up at one end. As the kids looked for seats in the stands, the lights went down and a roar from the crowd went up.

A man appeared on the screen. He was slightly built, with thick graying hair, tinted lab goggles, and a white lab coat. He was humming a crazy little tune and tinkering at a computer. He stopped, stood up, and looked at the camera. "I am Dr. Mee," he proclaimed in a thick Korean accent. "I am the founder and CEO of Mee Corp. When I was your age—as young as my little warrior Ines is now—I used to read novels of swords and sorcery. My father criticized me harshly. We lived in Seoul, Korea. He noted, quite rightly, that the books I read were all set in England. He said I should create a new place for fantasy. But I was not a writer, so I started an electronics company. The venture did not go well, at least at first. Then I took a business trip to the island of Jamaica, and there I had an idea. I fell in love with the land and its myths. The motto of Jamaica is Out of Many, One People. I thought, here is a place where

I can find the fantasies that all people share. And Xamaica was born."

Dr. Mee vanished from the screen and the crowd cheered.

Eli looked puzzled. "That was an old speech."

"How do you know?" Dylan asked.

"Let's just say I follow the company. Notice how he didn't say anything about the tournament?"

"First you tell me you hate Xamaica—now you say you follow news about Mee Corp.? What other stuff are you hiding?"

"Me, hiding? Speaking of which, Emma said you figured out what's behind your seizures. So what is it?"

Dylan didn't answer.

A new face had appeared on the screen: Ines Mee. The crowd cheered even louder.

"I know, right? On behalf of Mee Corp. and my dear old dad, welcome to the Tournament of Xamaica! We've chosen the best forty-four players in New Rock, based on your online scores. Here's how this is going to work. There's going to be a countdown, and then everyone can log on. This is a tag team match—you can pair up with friends or someone who is randomly assigned. Whichever pair is left standing is the winner of the Tournament of Xamaica! And I will personally give them the Grand Major Triple-Secret Prize! This is gonna be beyond awesome! Get ready for the forty-four Game Changers!"

A list of disclaimers quickly scrolled across the screen:

Children under the age of sixteen years old should only play Xamaica with parental permission ... Mee Corp. is not responsible for heart attacks, seizures, brain freezes, wedgies, or charley horses experienced during play . . . If children go missing while playing Xamaica please contact local law enforcement authorities and don't blame Mee Corp. because lots of kids disappear every year and it's unfair to blame video games for everything.

"Wouldn't it be boss if we both made it?" Eli said to Dylan. "We could be a team!"

"But you hardly even play the game!"

"You never know."

Ines was reading the list, which wasn't alphabetical, probably to build tension and keep people guessing. First up was a tall girl named Sarah, then this kid Rawley, then two brothers, Justin and Devin, then a brother and sister, C.J. and Sasha. Players heard their names and went down to their places in the spotlights. Some kids turned out not to be in the building when their names were called. Their spots were quickly and eagerly filled. After five minutes or so, only three empty spotlights were left.

"*The next lucky kid is—Chad Worthington!*" Ines announced.

Chad's beefy freckled face appeared on the big screen. He was dressed in a sweatshirt with a logo of a tree and a bird baring its claws—the Fighting Bird logo of Asgard Prep, a super-exclusive private school on the good side of town.

"Chad used to go to private school before his dad became superintendent of public schools," Eli pointed out. "I'm sure if his dad ever leaves his high-paying government gig, Chad will go right back to Asgard and all his rich buddies."

Chad gave high-fives and chest-bumps to some of his fellow Fighting Birds and took his place in the spotlight.

"Two more shots," Eli said.

Dylan felt like he couldn't breathe.

"The next lucky contestant: Elizondo Niall Marquez!"

The crowd went crazy again, and Dylan's jaw dropped as he looked at Eli, who just grinned and wheeled himself down to his spotlight.

There was one spot left. Would Dylan get it? Or had Mee Corp. uncovered his secret?

Ines smiled. *"And the final Game Changer is . . ."*

CHAPTER THREE

"*Ariel November!*" Ines announced.

The crowd cheered wildly.

Dylan felt his heart shrink three sizes.

He was finished. He hadn't been picked. Game over.

The world was a blur. Eli was saying something. Emma was shaking her head.

He had been fooling himself. Of course he wasn't a Game Changer! Nothing good ever happened to him. He was just another middle school loser. And now it was time for him to go home to his loserdom, his epic fail life, his kitchenette of cockatoos, and his urine-flavored lemonade bought in bulk. This time he'd drink the whole friggin' glass and if he was lucky it would kill him.

"*Ariel?*" Ines called out. "*Mr. or Ms. November? Going once, going twice . . .*"

The crowd murmured. Ariel November, whoever he or she was, wasn't there.

Ines stroked her long black hair. "*No worries . . . We'll just move on to our alternate . . . Dylan Rudee!*"

The crowd roared again. Dylan didn't know what to think. Did they really call his name?

"*Dylan, come on down!*"

His name! He *was* somebody. He was one of the best gamers in town. He thought of all the kids at school who called him nerd or loser or Loopy or worse. Maybe they were watching him on TV. He finally had one thing that he did well and it was games. And not only that, he had a way of playing this particular game that nobody else had. Then a note of doubt echoed through Dylan's head—what if he really wasn't one of the best? What if he was really just a sneaky kid with inside info?

"C'mon, Dylan," Emma cheered. "Go on down!"

Dylan couldn't feel his legs, but somehow he was moving. Everything seemed like one of those dreams where you know you're dreaming. He came down from the stands into the spotlight and saw his face on the big screen; in front of him he saw Eli smiling.

"Sweet!" Eli shouted. "Sweeeeeeeeet!"

Just then, Chad threw an elbow that caught Dylan in the nose and knocked him down. He tasted blood in his mouth. The crowd, which saw the hit on the screen, let out a gasp.

"Man up, Loopy—'cause I'm taking you down!" Chad barked. "That's right, I said it." Suddenly aware that he was on camera, he mugged for the crowd. The gasps turned to cheers. He chewed hard on his gum, blew a bubble, then let loose an Olympic-sized fart. The crowd loved it. "I got my swagger back!" he boomed.

Dylan scrambled to his feet. The cheap shot returned him to reality. As he stumbled into his spotlight, his left nostril was leaking blood. He couldn't play Xamaica like this; he thought maybe his nose was broken.

"Shhhhh. Lean forward, not back. You have to give the blood a place to go."

Emma had come up behind him. She put her pirate doll against his nose; he hadn't even noticed that she had brought it with her, but the darn thing made an excellent sponge. Emma pinched Dylan's nose bridge, then rolled up the doll's tiny felt hat and slipped it into his left nostril, stopping the bleeding.

"I-I-I didn't know you knew how to do that," Dylan stammered.

"There are a lot of things about me you don't know," Emma smiled.

"*Gracias por tu ayuda!*" Eli said. "That's a good woman!"

"She's a nine-year-old *girl*," Dylan fired back. "And she carries around a pirate doll."

Emma crossed her arms. The doll was a sore spot—Chad and his boys had stolen it once, and the whole

GAME WORLD

episode was kind of a disaster. "This isn't about me. If we lose the apartment, do you really think social services will let the Professor keep us? You *have* to win that prize."

"No pressure, huh?" Dylan muttered, as Emma returned to the stands.

A countdown appeared on the big screen: *10, 9, 8, 7, 6, 5, 4, 3, 2, 1!*

Naturally, Dylan and Eli chose each other as teammates. To start the game, a player had to say two and a half simple words:

"It's on!" Dylan yelled.

The game had begun. Xamaica's technology was a trade secret: users normally signed up online, and without a controller or any visible hardware, the game was transmitted into the field of vision of each of the players. Users were only faintly visible beneath their avatars. One time, Dylan remembered, Emma had tried the game out and she only had one comment afterward: *"Any sufficiently advanced technology is indistinguishable from magic.* Arthur C. Clarke." He hated to admit it, but she was so right. Now, playing the game, Dylan looked out onto a tropical land shrouded by a low mist. Of course, he was only viewing a video image, but it seemed totally real. Images of what the players were seeing were projected on the big screens for the crowd.

An orange sun and two pale moons glowed in the blue sky. This is what he loved about Xamaica: it was fantastical and yet so real. It was a world so welcoming it made him want to leave his own.

A player couldn't choose his or her avatar. Dylan had filled out an online form that had asked all sorts of weird questions, including, *Was your great-great-grandaunt left-handed?* and, *Have you ever eaten a plantain tart under a full moon?* and, *What's life all about anyway?* Dylan had no idea why they needed to know those things, and he'd left half the answers blank. But soon after, an avatar was assigned to him that was supposed to reflect what he was about. Since Dylan's avatar was a duppy, it looked like him, only a little transparent. But it had many powers. As a spirit-creature, he was a shape-shifter and a mimic—for brief bursts, he could take on the powers of any magical beast in Xamaica. He could shoot fire like a Rolling Calf, even fly like an Iron Lion—a creature with a lion body, a human face, and huge metallic butterfly wings.

In Xamaica, thanks to the special powers he had, people called Dylan the Duppy Defender. It had a better ring than Loopy.

Dylan looked around to get his bearings. Right beside him was Eli—his avatar was a Rolling Calf, kind of like a Minotaur that's on fire but never gets burned. When Rolling Calves stampeded they were an unstoppable force. Eli scraped the ground with his hoofs, throwing off sparks. His tail lashed back and forth, trailing flames and smoke. Fire blew from his nostrils. Dylan liked Eli this way.

There were forty-two other avatars in the contest, including a Steel Donkey, half-shark half-vulture Luscas, and a couple slinky Dlos (part-snake, part-human, mostly trouble). They were gathered in the field of combat, a large grassy plain fenced in by palm trees. Dylan had never seen so many magical beasts—it was a fire-breathing, shape-shifting, wind-walking, magical mystery melee.

"Okay, I have a plan." Eli's voice sounded bigger, more bullish, when he was playing the game.

"Not again," groaned Dylan, whose own game voice was distant and echoey, like something rattling around in an attic. "Is this new plan anything like what you pulled in the JV football locker room?"

"Dude—it's not like the super glue didn't come out eventually."

"So what do you have this time?"

"Teamwork."

"Teamwork? That's the plan?"

"It's the Fellowship of the Ring. Harry Potter doesn't get anything done without his *amigos*. The Narnia kids have each other's back. If you want to survive a fantasy situation, you have to roll with a crew. We're the real Game Changers, man! These other brothers are just playing!"

"So we do everything together? Coordinate every attack?"

"Exactly. Most of these clowns are working together for the first time, or they're in it for themselves. We work together, we got a shot."

Dylan figured they had more than a shot, because he had a secret, a way to game the game that nobody else knew. He cupped his hand over his mouth to cover his lips. Many video games had cheat codes—secret ways of gaining access to new levels that were known only to a few. Dylan had stumbled onto the ultimate cheat code for Xamaica—a secret word he only had to say once out loud to unlock and multiply the powers of his avatar. He whispered it now, to himself, and his avatar became supercharged.

About half the competitors went down in the first few seconds. The Luscas were pretty vicious. There was a pair of them and they worked well as a team. They circled the air like flying sharks and swooped down on their victims, seizing them with squidlike tentacles. They were merciless—a couple kids whose avatars were Wata Mamas, seal-like creatures as bulky and as useless as waterlogged mattresses, never had a chance. The last things they saw were six rows of teeth diving down on them from the air. Dylan thought that was a pretty grim way to get offed, even if it was just a video game.

Eli was good at this combat stuff. As a Rolling Calf, he was one of the most powerful creatures. He burned like a forest fire without the forest, and after he took out a couple zombies, nobody else wanted to come near him. His attacks were a one-two punch: he'd throw flames first and trample over anything that was left, which was usually just ashes. Dylan was his advance man, snooping out opponents hiding behind ferns or in the branches of banana trees. With his enhanced powers, nobody could stop him.

"Sweet!" Eli said to Dylan. "You're a beast!"

Meanwhile, two Seven-Tailed Lizards were doing some damage. Each of their tails could cause an earthquake—and they had fourteen tails between them, each one covered, naturally, in Richter scales. Other avatars were getting crushed by the tremors the two creatures were setting off. Eli couldn't even get close to them because the ground kept giving way. For a while it looked like the lizards were going to win the battle in a rout.

But, as it turned out, the lizards weren't much of a team. They kept squabbling with each other about which avatars to go after next. Eventually they began to chase after each other's tails. That was the end of the tale of the Seven-Tailed Lizards.

There was one other Loopy in the fight. Anjali was an Airavata—an oversized elephant with nine trunks and too many tusks to count. When she tooted those trunks she sounded like that French horn she was always playing. She was paired with a floppy Wata Mama. Anjali used her trunks to pull the vulturous Luscas out of the sky—but they ended up falling right on top of her and her partner. They were all knocked out of the battle and trunks, teeth, and dorsal fins went flying. The crash took out the nearby Steel Donkey, which gave a last tinny bray before collapsing in a heavy metal crash. Just to be nice, Dylan and Eli saved a few sweetly useless Wata Mamas from getting crushed. The creatures, who it turned out weren't even players, bleated and waddled away toward a stream.

A Dlo whose partner had gone down early was mounting a challenge. He was slithering in and out of holes in the ground, striking quickly, and slipping away. Dylan couldn't figure out which hole he was going to pop out of next. The Dlo was taking out the field one by one, and nobody could do anything about it.

Eli had a solution. He blew fire into one hole until smoke came out of all the rest. Pretty soon the Dlo was smoked out. Hacking and hissing, he was an easy target.

Soon, Eli and Dylan were one of two pairs left. They were up against Chad and his partner, Ivan, who were both towering Moongazers. Even with Dylan's supersized powers, this was real trouble.

Moongazers were among the most fearsome creatures in Xamaica. Because their bearlike bodies were made of mist they were hard to get ahold of. Their claws, however, were long and sharp and could tear through wood, metal—and the hides of other beasts.

"End of the road, Dylan. That's right, I said it." The twin Moongazers looked exactly alike, but there was no mistaking Chad's typically insulting tone.

"Teamwork," Eli cautioned. "Don't let him bait you."

"That's right, Loopy, listen to the cripple!" Chad barked.

"Shut up!" Dylan warned, even as Eli tried to hold him back.

"Make me!" Chad caught a Wata Mama sunning itself near a stream and flung it by the tail.

Dylan caught the poor creature, put it down safely, and flew at Chad in a rage—but then he remembered the other Moongazer. He just ducked a swipe from the creature's massive claws. He wasn't, however, able to dodge the beast's backhand, which knocked him back twenty feet. Dylan was a spirit creature, so blows like that usually went through him. But there was something about the Moongazer's vaporous body that allowed it to have an effect on noncorporal beings.

Chad howled and took two menacing strides forward to finish the job.

A blast of fire shot between the Moongazers and Dylan. Dylan scrambled behind a rock where Eli was waiting, his eyes flickering with flame. "Teamwork—remember!"

"Teamwork's cool," Dylan panted. "But we need to change the playbook."

His extra cheat-code powers were wearing off—they never lasted long. He needed a new approach. As a duppy, Dylan could shape-shift into any creature. But what form should he pick?

"I need to turn into something that can fight that thing," Dylan said.

"Like what?" Eli asked.

"A Rolling Calf?"

"Dude—my fire blast barely fazed him."

"An Iron Lion?"

"Seriously? You're not gonna be able to hold that form long."

The Moongazers were sniffing around the rock. They were closing in. What form should he choose? Then it hit him. *If you can't beat 'em . . .*

Dylan turned into a Moongazer.

"Sweet!" Eli said, picking up on the plan.

It was a powerful beast, so he wasn't going to be able to maintain the shift, but he should be able to do it long enough. He charged.

"What are you trying to pull, Loopy?" said one of the Moongazers. Based on the sneer in his voice, Dylan figured that one was Chad.

Dylan tackled the other one. They wrestled and rolled on the ground and it was impossible to tell who was who—which was exactly what Dylan was counting on.

Chad looked confused. After hesitating, he attacked

anyway. One of the Moongazers howled in pain. By mistake, Chad had done in his partner.

Working together, Eli and Dylan handled their opponent quickly. Dylan blocked Chad's escape while Eli fireblasted his gaseous body into smoke. You know how a lit match can air out a room after someone has let one rip? Same principle.

"You lose," Dylan said to Chad. "That's right, I said it."

Dylan and Eli had won the Tournament of Xamaica.

Eli bumped his fist against Dylan's. "Dude—that was epic! How did you know he'd attack the wrong Moongazer?"

"I didn't. But I got a tip this morning about the kind of guy Chad is. So I figured he'd attack first and ask questions later. I guess we just had to get a little lucky."

The twin wounds across Dylan's chest began to ache.

"What's the matter?" Eli asked.

"It's those scratches. I don't know why they're hurting so bad."

"How bad could it be?"

"Ever put the tip of your tongue against a frozen metal pole? Imagine doing that with your bare chest—and then ripping it away."

"Gross. Let's get out of here. Game over."

Xamaica faded away. Then Dylan and Eli were in the arena and the crowd was cheering all around them. A group of uniformed Xamaica officials came out and ushered the two boys to a circular stage in the center of the arena while the crowd yelled louder.

"So what's the Grand Major Triple-Secret Prize?" Dylan asked.

"It better be straight-up cash," Eli said. "If only the

dinero in the game was real! Then we'd be talking serious money."

The circular stage descended beneath the floor of the arena. Emma was waiting there, clapping and waving her bloodstained pirate doll. Dylan, Eli, and Emma were hustled into a hall, through a door, and outside the building. Their escorts left abruptly, slamming the door behind them.

The kids were standing there in an empty alley as a light rain began falling.

Eli scowled. "Well, this sucks canal water. What about the friggin' Grand Major Triple-Secret Prize? If my wheelchair rusts, I'm gonna be pissed."

At that moment, a black stretch limo pulled up. A tinted back window rolled down. Someone was clapping. Dylan recognized the dark gaze and the peek-a-boo hairstyle.

"That was beyond awesome!" Ines Mee purred. "Now it gets hard."

CHAPTER FOUR

The limo raced down the slick streets as the rain kept falling. Dylan, Eli, and Emma were sitting in the spacious backseat of the car across from Ines. Like an online video that hasn't quite downloaded, Dylan's brain was still buffering after winning the tournament.

"Your hair is . . . amazing," Emma complimented Ines, to break the unsettling silence and because her hair really was amazing.

"I know, right?" Ines stroked the glossy locks that flowed shimmering over the right side of her face. "It's easy to maintain; the real hassle is flying my styling staff in every weekend from Dubai."

"Where's your camera crew?" Emma asked.

"I gave them the evening off. I have important things to do tonight—"

"So when are we going to get our prize?" Eli interrupted.

Ines looked at Eli like she was noticing a stray thread on a designer dress. "So that's your famous slanket. I saw it in your file."

"It's a snuglet," Eli shot back.

"I know that—Mee Corp. owns the company that makes them. Or we did. We may have sold them off. Something about extreme flammability. Nothing you need to worry about unless you smoke in bed, use a toaster oven, or get an extremely high fever."

"And why do you have a file on me exactly?"

"How interesting!" Ines said, clapping. "That's exactly what your file said you'd ask!"

Ines suddenly leaned forward and the tinted glass divider between the driver's seat and the passenger seat slid down. "We're being followed," she informed the driver.

Dylan looked out the back window and saw a pair of red lights. Then he realized they weren't coming from the car. The motorist behind them was wearing a dark hood that hid his face, though Dylan could see one thing: he had glowing red eyes.

Dylan swallowed hard. "Who's chasing us?"

"Let me worry about that, kitten," Ines soothed.

She leaned forward and whispered a series of directions to the driver. "Buckle up," Ines commanded the kids. "But don't worry—the same thing happened on the twelfth season of my show. We were in Venice, and we were being chased by gondolas, but the situation was basically the same."

The car accelerated and everyone was thrown back in his or her seat. Eli's glasses flew off and as the vehicle jerked around, Dylan stepped on them and felt something crunch. Emma picked up the glasses, which looked fine, and handed them to Eli.

"*Gracias*," Eli said, sliding his glasses back on. He turned to Ines. "I've had enough of this crap! When do we get our cash prize?"

"Adventure is the prize!" Ines declared, her black eyes blazing. "Mee Corp. has files on *both* of you. You're now the best Xamaica players in the region. If you've seen my show, you know what I live for. It's what we're all about to go on. Three words: Greatest. Adventure. Ever."

"You mean we're going to play Xamaica again?" Dylan asked.

"No," Ines replied. "We're going there—for real."

"Seriously?" Eli said. "You're seriously serious?"

"I'm beyond serious. You've made it to the forty-third level. Now we're going to the forty-fourth."

"So you think magic . . . is real?" Eli said.

"I believe Xamaica is a real place. That's why I think we can go there. Don't be a hater—I need you to trust it's true."

"Yo, here's what's true: you are a total nut job," Eli said. "No offense."

"I believe!" Emma said to Ines. "Picasso said, *Everything you can imagine is real.*"

"I just don't know," Dylan muttered. He wondered if Ines knew about his cheat code.

Ines was unflustered. "By the end of tonight," she said. "You. Will. Believe."

The limo pulled into the Mee Mansion and the vast gate came down, shutting them in.

"Will that gate keep out the freaky dude with the red eyes?" Dylan asked.

"We have a pretty tight security system," Ines answered. "Now and again a mailman or a Girl Scout gets electrocuted, but it's a price I'm willing to pay."

On the outside at least, the Mee Mansion looked more like an ancient castle than a modern-day home. It had stained-glass windows, gargoyles mounted on the walls, and even a couple of drawbridges. Dylan imagined it was the kind of place where a mad scientist and an evil wizard could spend some quality time together. "This is incredible."

Ines shrugged. "Everything isn't everything. I sent the help home for the day so we can have some privacy."

Everyone exited the limo and Ines led them to a large stone door. She pressed a button and it slid open. The inside of the Mee Mansion was even wilder than the outside. The exterior was brooding and medieval; the interior was shadowy and futuristic, in a retro kind of way. Dylan thought it was sort of like what people imagined the future might have looked like a couple generations ago; the place felt modern and antique at the same time. There were cameras and mirrors and video screens everywhere. It was hard to tell what was a door, what was a window, and what was a hallway.

"They call this the Mee Mansion," Ines told them. "I call it Uncanny Valley."

"You named your home?" Eli scoffed. "We've got cats at my place that we haven't gotten around to naming."

"Doesn't it get lonely in this big house?" Emma asked, her voice echoing a bit.

"Yes and no," Ines said, stroking her own hair. "Me and dear old Dad spend a lot of time together, so it's all good."

She led them through a room with an Olympic-sized swimming pool, another with Olympic-sized pianos, and then into a spherical room with a massive dark globe in the middle.

"Is this where you plan world domination?" Eli asked.

Ines smiled. "Oh, we're beyond that, kitten. Mee Corp. has factories on every continent—including Antarctica . . ."

"Spare us the infomercial," Eli said.

Emma walked over to the globe.

"Don't touch that! It's personal . . ." Ines began.

Too late—the globe lit up. A 3-D image of a child—age seven?—appeared above the continent of Europe, somewhere near maybe Azerbaijan. *Greetings, Ines. This is Artur from Shemakha. You'll never believe . . .*" the child started to say.

Ines put her hand on the globe and the image vanished.

"What was that about?" Eli asked.

"I told you, it's personal," Ines said. After an awkward silence, she continued: "We have a lot of rooms—a piano room, a cheese room, a tapestry room. If I had to explain them all, we'd be here all night and never get to where we're going."

"A cheese room?" Eli asked. "Is that a thing?"

"Duh—to go with the cracker room," Ines replied. "Follow me."

After a long walk, Ines led them into a huge chamber in which the walls, ceilings, and floors were all a brilliant white. "Welcome to the game room," Ines announced. "This is where we'll go to the forty-fourth level."

On one end of the vast room was mounted a black tablet, a little bit bigger than a Bible, that looked like it was made from solid rock. "What's that?" Eli asked.

"That's the master portal to Xamaica," Ines explained. "The tablet was my father's greatest invention. It's the nexus for every Xamaica gaming experience. Once we link to it, because we're so close, we should have the strongest possible connection to Xamaica."

Eli snorted. "What's in it for us?"

"Xamaica is filled with treasures. Springs of liquid silver. Mangoes filled with gold. A sorceress with a magic book that contains all the wealth of the world between its covers."

Eli's green eyes got even bigger than usual. "All the wealth of the world? Sweet!"

"So how do we link up to this portal?" Dylan asked.

"Well, there's a hitch," Ines cautioned.

Eli sighed. "There always is."

CHAPTER FIVE

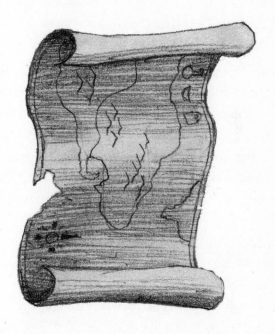

Ines held up a sheet of yellowed parchment. Different feelings and emotions—curiosity, anticipation, anxiety— kept flashing across her face like vehicles with their high beams on zooming by on a dark highway.

"What's that?" Eli asked.

"If I knew I wouldn't have to ask you," Ines said.

Emma took a closer look. It was a map of the edge of an island with three faint symbols on it. "It's a code."

"If we can decode it, will the tablet turn on?" Dylan asked.

"Obviously that's the point," Eli said. "But I don't know why they have to make it so difficult."

"There's a perfectly reasonable explanation . . ." Emma began.

"Here she goes," Dylan moaned.

"Monks used to put dots or spaces between words when they were copying books," Emma said. "But between the second and seventh centuries they stopped. Wanna know why?"

"Not really, but I guess you're going to tell us anyway," Dylan said.

"Leaving no space between words made books hard to read. It forced people to pay attention to what was really being said. Whoever made this parchment wants us to focus."

"Thanks for the history lesson," Dylan scoffed. "Ines—did your dad use this parchment? Why can't we just ask him what it means?"

"Yeah—and where is he anyway?" Eli added.

"Let me worry about that," Ines replied. "Nobody knows more about Xamaica than us. We need this portal if we're going to get to Xamaica for real. This code is what opens up the portal . . . So what do these symbols mean? Anybody? Anything?"

Dylan peered at the parchment. The top image was an oval with a kind of bar jutting out of the top, the next appeared to be a smile, and the last looked like a lock without a keyhole. "Well, the first image could be a key."

"I thought that too," Ines said. "There are 256 doors in

Uncanny Valley, and 145 keys. None of them opens anything in this room."

"We're being too literal," Emma said.

"So when is a key not a key?" Eli asked.

The kids stood around for a bit and Ines began to hum that same crazy tune that her dad did in the video. Dylan smiled and turned to Ines. "You have a tapestry room, a cheese room—and a piano room, right?"

"Yes, why?"

"Your humming gave me an idea. I'm going to need help."

Dylan and Ines pushed one of the grand pianos into the room.

"A piano key!" Emma laughed.

Ines ran her hands over the keys. "What do we play?"

"It's gotta be some song that means something to your family," Emma said.

"What's that melody your dad's always humming?" Dylan asked Ines.

"He used to play it when I was a baby," she answered. "I don't know the name."

Ines hummed a simple little tune that was like really sad carnival music.

Emma sat at the piano. "I've got nearly perfect pitch. I hear something once, I can play it."

She played the tune with her left hand. Nothing happened for a few moments, then all at once the black tablet flashed like the sun emerging from an eclipse. The kids were momentarily blinded, and shut their eyes. When they opened them again, the black tablet had vanished, and the white room was gone. "It's on," Ines breathed. "It's really on."

Xamaica was suddenly all around them, brighter and bolder and realer than ever, like going from standard to HD to whatever is a quantum leap past that.

Dylan turned to Emma. "Time for you to scram."

"Are you kidding? I'm not going to let you go alone!"

"*Let* me?"

"You got through the tournament. But you need a doctor, Dylan. You nearly—"

"Whoa—medical issues?" Ines broke in. "Should I have my lawyer draft a release form? If you get hurt I don't want you suing Mee Corp!"

"Dude—are you gonna tell me what this is all about?" Eli asked.

"He's not supposed to play!" Emma said. "The doctor . . ."

"I'm calling my lawyer," Ines announced. "What time is it in Zurich?"

"Stop it—everyone!" Dylan shouted. "I'm doing this, okay?"

"Then I'm coming too," Emma said. "You have to let me help—"

"No!" Dylan barked. "Absolutely not!"

"Dude—c'mon, chill," Eli said. "She did stop your nosebleed with a pirate doll. That's got to count for something."

"She shouldn't be carrying that thing around! Especially with the trouble it's caused us!"

"You shouldn't blame her for that pirate party! That was all on Chad and his goons!"

"Don't you get it?" Dylan shouted. "I don't need Viral Emma following me around."

"Stop calling me that!" Emma shot back. "I'm just trying to help you!"

"I don't need your help! You act like you can fix everything—but you can't! You're not my mom. We never even really knew Mom! She could be some evil crazy person!"

"Maybe I'm not Mom. But some part of me is. I mean, she's the root of our family tree, right? But the way you're acting, would you even recognize Mom if you met her? 'Cause I'm your sister, I'm standing right in front of you, and you don't know me at all."

"Get out! Go play with your pirate doll!"

Emma seemed close to tears as she stared right at Dylan. *"The only journey is the one within.* Rainer Maria Rilke. Think about it." She sulked off, clutching her doll.

Eli shook his head at Dylan disapprovingly. "Harsh."

Dylan crossed his arms. "Necessary."

"You want to go get her?" Eli asked.

"Definitely not," Dylan said. "I don't care where she goes. Let's do this."

Ines's expression grew serious. "So now it begins," she said. "To the forty-fourth level and beyond!"

CHAPTER SIX

The kids' avatars appeared. Ines was a metal-winged Iron Lion, Eli was a fire-eyed Rolling Calf, and Dylan, as usual, was himself, but a little more ghostly.

Eli stomped his hooves, throwing up sparks. "So what do the other symbols mean?"

"We'll have to figure them out en route," Ines said, her game voice a mix of purrs and growls. "They point the way to the forty-fourth level. If we can uncover what they mean, we'll make it through. For now, let's just go as far as we can."

They quickly went through level after level. When nobody was looking, Dylan whispered his cheat code to himself and multiplied his powers. Opposition withered away.

"I haven't seen anything that reminds me of the second two symbols," Eli said.

"Wait for it," Ines replied. "Those images are the key to unlocking the final level."

They journeyed through the misty reaches of Xamaica. They climbed blue mountains that had never been scaled, and swam down purple rivers whose waters had never been swum. Eli and Ines offered up advice—secret trails, hidden passages, and the like. And Dylan used all his power to keep the party moving along. But they didn't run into anything that seemed to have a connection to the symbols.

"The map seemed to show a lock without a keyhole," Eli said. "Maybe that means there's no solution."

"You said the same thing after the French midterm," Dylan said.

"Exactly—I got every question right and they still failed me."

"Do you think maybe answering in Spanish had anything to do with your grade?"

"I'm proud of my Spanish heritage, *amigo*," Eli said. "*Viva la Revolución!*"

Ines sighed. "Let's just keep going."

So they went on. The adventure points were pouring out like coins spitting out of a slot machine that had hit the jackpot. Soon they came to a place where the land met the sea.

"This is it!" Ines exclaimed. "The end of the forty-third level."

"I can't believe we're already here!" Eli said. "I thought the forty-fourth level was one of those things corporations make up to keep you buying products, like static cling or morning breath!"

"Dude, morning breath is a real thing," Dylan said. "So is static cling."

"Really?" Eli said. "Well, that explains my problems with girls and with laundry."

Dylan looked around. "Hey—I got here once. I carved my name on a tree."

"It's as far as anyone has gotten," Ines said. "The question is, what does the next symbol mean?"

"When is a smile not a smile?" Eli wondered out loud.

"Maybe it's not a smile," Dylan speculated. "Maybe it's something else."

"Maybe it's laughing at us," Eli said.

"Come on, think!" Ines demanded. "These symbols are the opposite of what they look like. This looks like a mouth. What else could it be?"

"What else has a mouth?" Eli said. "A shark?"

"Too easy," Dylan replied. "What about a bottle? Or a cave?"

Eli started chuckling. "We're right next to the answer."

They were standing on the bank of a river.

Starting from the river's mouth, they followed it farther inland.

"We still have to figure out the last clue," Ines said.

"We could use Emma's help right about now," Eli mumbled.

"We don't need her," Dylan shot back. "Stay on point. We can do this."

At last, they came to a waterfall. But it wasn't just any waterfall—it was the mother and father and maybe the aunt and uncle of all waterfalls. It was so high Dylan couldn't see the top, which extended into the clouds. And where it crashed into a river below, it exploded into golden spray—it was the source of all the mist in the area. It was a column of crashing water connecting heaven and earth. And the water was gold.

"The forty-fourth level is behind the falls," Ines said. "How do we get to it?"

"When is a lock not a lock?" Eli said.

"When it's an air lock?" Dylan ventured.

"Dude, what about a leg lock—y'know, like in wrestling?" Eli said. "Not that I would know anything about wrestling or legs."

"The Erie Canal," Dylan said. "There are locks on that."

"I got a mule her name is Sal . . ." Eli sang.

". . . fifteen miles on the Erie Canal!" Dylan finished.

"I am gonna put both of you in a headlock unless you shut up and focus," Ines said.

The kids stood there for the longest time but nobody had any more ideas.

Ines stomped her foot. "I can't believe we went this far, only to come up short!"

She tugged at her curtain of hair in frustration. Dylan and Eli looked at each other. Eli nodded and Dylan walked over to her. As usual, her black hair cascaded down the right side of her face. Dylan reached out and Ines jerked back a bit.

"When is a lock not a lock?" Dylan said.

Ines stared at him—and then smiled. "When it's a lock of hair," she said.

He brushed back the lock of hair that always covered her right eye. In the image before them, the curtain of waterfall moved aside. "My dad used to brush my hair back like that," Ines said. "I was connected to the game all along."

Eli pointed. "Look—behind the water, something is carved onto those rocks."

"It's an inscription," Ines observed. "*There is no way—but The Way.*"

"Some of the lines have been struck out," Dylan added. "But I think I can make out a few. *Give your life—and you will find it.* That sounds dangerous."

Eli looked closer. "It's signed or something. Look at the bottom—those are probably initials. *The Inklings—H.G., J.K., C.S., and . . .*"

Ines unconsciously brushed her hair back in front of her face. "No!" Dylan shouted.

It was too late: water began to gush from the ceiling onto the floor. The images were suddenly real, and the chamber quickly began filling up with water. The children were caught in the current and started to be swept around the room. Just then, the door opened.

"What's going . . . oh!"

Emma had entered the room and the torrent had taken her by surprise. Now she was caught up in the raging waters too.

"Brush your hair back!" Dylan shouted over the sound of the surge.

"I tried that!" Ines said.

"Kill the power!"

"What?" Ines asked.

"He's right!" Eli hollered. "We've got to turn off the tablet!"

Ines dove down and surfaced a few moments later near a far wall, coughing up water. She slammed her hand on an emergency panel. The room went white—except for a rectangular area where the tablet had hung at the far end of the chamber. The water began to drain from the room like when a stopper is pulled in a tub. The flood was being sucked into the rectangular space where the tablet had been.

"Hold on to something—or we'll be drained away too!" Dylan yelled.

Ines latched onto a door handle, Eli wrapped his arms around a table leg, and Dylan grabbed onto the grand piano. But Emma had been caught by surprise.

"Dylan—help!" she cried.

The water was almost all sucked out of the room. Emma was in a swirling pool being pulled into the portal. "Emma!" yelled Dylan, letting go of the piano and splashing toward her.

Too late—her face disappeared in the deluge and a beastly roar filled the room that sounded like the combination of a breaking dam and an avalanche.

The room was dry now and the tablet had reappeared and swelled to the size of a door. Its flat surface showed the image of rushing water. Emma was gone.

CHAPTER SEVEN

L ike most twelve-year-olds, Dylan had gone his whole life without ever seeing magic.

Sure he had observed card tricks, watched palm readings, and a couple times he had seen street magicians performing for spare change. But seeing real magic was completely different—it made special effects in movies seem totally un-special. Real magic is more than an experience for the eyes. True wizardry wakes up the body and puts the senses on notice as they struggle to make sense of what's going on. All of Dylan's senses were awake and screaming for explanations, like baseball players shouting at umpires.

"This isn't happening, right?" Dylan asked Ines. "Tell me this is a prank!"

Ines's face was flushed.

Eli dragged himself back onto his wheelchair and rolled over to the weird opening. He reached out a hand and when he pulled it back it was dripping water. "The portal—if that's what to call this—is still open."

"This is a sick joke," Dylan cried. "Let's jump in the portal and find her!"

"Whoa—hold on and think about this," Ines said, recovering a bit.

"You're filming this for TV—is that it?" Dylan said.

Ines shook her head. "This is not a TV show. I don't know where your sister went."

"Things like this don't happen in New Rock!" Dylan yelled. "This can't be real!"

"Maybe we should call the cops," Ines said. "Or the coast guard."

"You told us that Xamaica was real!" Eli shouted. *"Greatest. Adventure. Ever.* Why weren't you better prepared?"

"This is magic!" Ines shot back. "How can you prepare for that?"

"This isn't happening!" Dylan moaned. "We've got to get my sister—now!"

"This better not be some corporate trick to cheat us from our prize!" Eli added.

"Will you shut up about the prize? This is about my sister!"

"You know how I feel about Emma! I just think the

spokesmodel here is hiding something! You can't trust a corporation, I'm telling you!"

"What about the red-eyed stalker guy?" Dylan asked. "Is he behind this?"

"He couldn't have gotten by security," Ines said. "We need help. Call 911!"

"I don't know if this is a game, a trick, or what, but there's no time to call anyone," Dylan said. "We don't know how long this portal will stay open. This has to be linked to the forty-fourth level. We're Xamaica's greatest players. If anyone can find her, it's us."

"Let's do this," Eli said. "I got your back, Dylan. Another mission for the Game Changers!"

Eli strapped himself securely into his wheelchair and gave Dylan a fist bump.

Ines paused for a moment in thought. "I started this— so I'm going too," she said at last. "But no group hugs or anything. This bromance thing you guys got going made me throw up in my mouth a little bit."

"You've got an heiress and a paraplegic as bodyguards," Eli said, putting up the hood of his snuglet. "What could possibly go wrong?"

Dylan wondered about that, and about the wounds on his chest. Maybe something in this game was out to kill him. He didn't know what it was but he was going to find out very soon. He just hoped he'd find his sister before whatever it was found him. *It's just a game,* he thought. *I'm not really here. This isn't happening.*

He took a step forward into the portal, Eli and Ines by his side.

BOOK TWO

THE GREAT WEB OF ANANCY

CHAPTER EIGHT

The roar of a waterfall filled their ears and they were submerged in liquid and gulping for air. Dylan had a vague sense he was plunging from somewhere high to somewhere down below.

The Professor had once taken Dylan and Emma to Niagara Falls. It wasn't a vacation or anything, she had a conference and couldn't afford a babysitter. After about five hours of bird lectures (including a ninety-minute symposium on molting), Emma and Dylan had gotten a chance to see the falls, and heard all about the daredevils who used to go over it in barrels. This was exactly like that only multiplied by skydiving and minus the barrel.

It was dark and they were tumbling down falls stretching from the clouds to the earth.

Suddenly they hit an invisible barrier and stopped falling. They seemed to be on the deck of a ship, but it was like nothing Dylan had ever seen. In fact, he could barely see it. Everything in the vessel was made of glass. But it was more than glass—upon close inspection, the stairs, the deck, everything was composed of some sort of hard crystalline substance that sparkled in the night sky. They were in an almost-invisible sailing ship, several hundred feet long, with a single mast in the center. The sails were made of a material that was lighter than a spider's web and could scarcely be seen. The sharp smell of citrus fruits and sea salt blew across the deck.

The ship began to drop. Not as quickly as the falls, but fast enough.

Eli gripped the wheels of his chair. "Dude—where are we?"

"No idea—but do you see any sign of my sister on this boat?"

Eli and Ines peered around the deck and Dylan leaned over the ship's railing. There was a name on the side of the vessel in nearly transparent letters: *BLACK STARR*.

"The *Black Starr*—I've heard of this ship," Dylan said. "Mom used to sing a lullaby about it to Emma—it's one of the few things I can remember. Something about the sea . . . it's coming back to me now. It's an old legend—it belongs to the pirate Ma Sinéad."

The ship was another piece of his parental puzzle. Of all the places in the world—or out of the world—Dylan never thought he'd find clues about his family here. He could feel the puzzle rearranging itself in his brain. Why would a pirate ditty stick in his head? And why was his mom singing a video game song? "We must be dreaming."

"Dude—dreams aren't multiplayer," Eli said.

The ship continued to plunge downward, keel first. They were hundreds of feet in the air and heading straight down the waterfall.

"We'd better strap ourselves in," Ines said.

They all looked around the deck until Eli found some rope. They tied themselves together and wrapped the end around the main mast. Then Eli pointed out a glowing red dot on the horizon. It was quickly joined by another, and very soon there was a swarm. Whatever the things were, they were approaching fast.

"Could that be . . . ?" Dylan began.

"Yup, it's the red-eyed stalker," Ines broke in. "Looks like he has pals."

"They're swarming like mosquitoes," Eli said.

"Could those be . . . Higues?" Dylan asked.

"You're right," Eli affirmed. "I've heard other players talk about them! I guess a real one was chasing the limo! They're like mosquitoes crossed with vampires."

"The mosquito part I can deal with," Ines shuddered. "But that vampire part is freaking me out. Can this boat go faster?"

"Chill," Eli said. "I thought you were used to adventures. It's basically all you do on that reality show of yours. I once saw you ride an elephant—sidesaddle."

"I saw you use a boa constrictor as a lasso," Dylan added.

"Whatever. I'd feel a lot more confident if we could actually see who was piloting our ship," Ines muttered.

"I think it's piloting itself," Eli said.

Ines began to run her hand along the ship's railing.

"What are you doing?" Eli asked.

"Looking for a lifeboat," Ines replied.

"To go where?"

They continued to sail down the waterfall into a wall of continual wet, like the air was full of firehoses. Dylan raised his arm and pointed—in a far corner of the sky, there loomed a shape the color of congealed blood. It was surrounded by swarms of Higues, but it soon outdistanced them. It was faster, stronger, bigger. And, unlike the Higues, it was catching up with the ship. In fact, it was on a collision course with the *Black Starr*.

"Do you think you can die in a dream?" Dylan asked.

"My grandma died in her sleep," Eli answered. "I always wondered what she was dreaming about. Maybe this is it."

"I'm officially freaking out," Ines declared.

From another corner of the sky, a second shape appeared. It was smaller, darker, faster, and sped toward the first. They were about to collide in midair above the ship. Then, louder than all thunder, the atmosphere echoed with the same soul-shaking roar Dylan had first heard when he was wounded on the chest and again when Emma vanished.

Everything went white.

Dylan woke up floating down a canal.

He was soaking wet. He staggered out of the warm

water, untangled himself from a length of frayed rope, and collapsed on the bank. He looked up to see the giant golden waterfall. Shards of crystal were scattered all around him. Had the *Black Starr* crashed?

Something had attacked them. He didn't quite know what it was, or why. Maybe it was some sort of guardian of the threshold, the same beast that had clawed his chest when he played the game. The doctors told him he'd had an episode. He sensed there was more to it. But he didn't know if it would strike again.

He felt a sharp sting against his cheek. He'd been cut by a piece of glass. All around him, he noticed that the shattered remains of the *Black Starr* were sliding along the ground, whizzing through the air, and colliding against one another, forming big pieces. It was as if the invisible ship was struggling to rebuild itself. A rough outline of the vessel was beginning to take shape. It was like watching a crystal form.

It was weird, but Dylan had other stuff to worry about. Where was his sister? Where were his friends? Where was he?

Then, at the base of a giant palm tree, he saw it: the letter *D*. Just where he had carved it when he was playing the game.

This had to be Xamaica. There was no question that this was the forty-fourth level. He had always thought of it as a dream world, but now that he was here, it felt as if it was his old world that had been a dream. Everything seemed bigger, richer, deeper than anything he had encountered in his previous life before this place. He was beyond the golden mists of the mountain regions. His senses seemed to be working for the first time in his life. This was no video game. He could feel this world. He could smell it. He could taste it.

Dylan began to run for joy. All those goons on the bus who called him Loopy and pushed him around and broke his stuff—he wished they could see him now. No, he was glad they couldn't, because he wanted this world, this feeling, this moment, all to himself. He felt like the people he had seen in books, or in movies, who had gone someplace nobody had ever been, somewhere everyone had always wanted to go, and they made it there despite all the haters saying they couldn't, like Earhart across the Atlantic, Armstrong on the moon, or Obama in the White House.

Dylan found himself sprinting quicker than he ever had—faster than a skateboard or a bike. Soon he was leaping in the air, running, jumping, and through a break in the trees sunlight washed over him. He saw a purple river, a green lake, and a white waterfall. He noticed a school of Wata Mamas frolicking in the river below. He could glimpse, beyond the hills, a procession of mountains, their peaks tipped by a green cloud.

The sky was a stunning shade of blue so blue it blew away his blues. Arching through the sky was something else: a huge spider web that stretched across the entire expanse, from one horizon to the other. Silvery strands sparkled in the sunlight. It both blended into the sky and stood out, depending on how the light caught it. It was tied down to the earth on the edges of the sky by four huge strands that must have been the size of ten thousand tree trunks. The web hadn't been visible when he played the game, perhaps because the mists obscured it.

This was a strange place. And his sister was lost and alone somewhere here. Dylan's joy swirled away, like a bubble bath going down the drain.

He couldn't just enjoy being in Xamaica. He had a mission—he had to find his sister.

A fury bubbled up in him, lava dripping over the lip of a volcano. Emma was always friggin' messing up his life. He gets invited to the Tournament of Xamaica, and she has to tag along. He goes to Ines Mee's mansion, and she has to butt in. She goads him about being a Game Changer, and when he finally gets on the list she tries to tell him it's too dangerous. It was bad enough having her in the same grade as him, taking the same tests. He used to be one of the best students in school, but now what was the point in trying so hard if he was just going to finish second to his freakishly tall rocket scientist sister? Now here he was, trying to get her out of a mess she should have never been in. This was *so* Emma it was unbelievable.

Then he felt mean for thinking these thoughts with his sister still MIA. But there was something cleansing about it, like when you pop a zit and all the pus squirts out. Yeah, sure, maybe he had a responsibility to rescue her, but that didn't mean he had to like it.

Anyway, none of this was real. It wasn't really happening. He closed his eyes. Maybe if he thought hard about his apartment, when he woke up his sister would be there.

Suddenly, two screams sounded across paradise.

He opened his eyes . . . Emma?

CHAPTER NINE

In a small vine-draped clearing, Dylan noticed an odd-looking black spider. The creature was unusual for several reasons. For one, the thing was the size of a dog—and not a poodle, a Great Dane. Plus, it was wearing a hat—a knit cap colored black, gold, and green, with dreadlocks tumbling out of the sides. On four of its eight legs, it wore shoes—all of them untied with laces dangling. On its back, instead of the hourglass-shaped spots some spiders have, it had two ivory markings like a woman's long-lashed eyes. They seemed to stare back at Dylan and he half expected them to blink.

Then he saw Ines and Eli, who were caught in a large

web that spanned the space between two trees and extended upward twice the length of Dylan's body. But the web's size was not the most unusual thing about it. What made it truly bizarre was the weird way it was all tied together. Instead of radiating out from a central point like a proper web, the strands of this ropey mess seemed to have been spun almost at random. Some were strung this way, others that way. Still others were rolled into balls, while others were twirled into curlicues. Some came down in diagonals, others hung in sad drooping arcs, while still others lay discarded on the ground like gray garden hoses.

Dylan was still considering this disaster of a web when the spider that had most likely made it looked at him, and when a creature with eight eyes looks right at you it's an intensely ophthalmological experience.

A giant spider? Really? What did he do to deserve this? How could this be happening to him? He was just a sixth grader from New Rock! The weirdness, the unfairness of the whole situation, was making him mad. How was he going to find his sister if eight-legged, wall-crawling monsters kept getting in his way?

Dylan decided it was time to unleash the Duppy Defender.

In the Xamaica game, Dylan could take on the powers of every magical beast in the land. This time he opted to draw on the abilities of a Chupacabra, a hunched lizardlike creature with spines on its back, a mouthful of fangs, and eyes that shoot lava. He whispered the cheat code and then prepared to unleash a molten blast at the spider.

Nothing happened.

What was wrong? What did he have to do to trigger his powers? Did he need more Xamaican sunlight? A spell of some sort? He didn't seem to have any special powers anymore, much less his enhanced abilities. He could run and jump and smell the flowers a bit better, and that was about it.

"None of our powers are working," Eli observed.

"And did I tell you I'm an arachnophobe?" Ines complained.

"In fact you did," Eli sighed. "Several times."

The spider took a step toward Dylan, or rather a tentative crawl.

Dylan grabbed a stick and jabbed it at the giant creature. He felt like a crossing guard waving a stop sign at a runaway truck. The spider grabbed the stick in its mandibles and crushed it before picking up Dylan in its front two legs. Dylan was eye to eye with the beast and his human eyes were totally outnumbered. Dylan squirmed. "Let me go!"

The monster stopped. A look of surprise passed over its face, or what Dylan imagined surprise would look like if an arachnid could register such a thing. It dropped Dylan onto the ferny forest floor.

"Mon, you can talk!" exclaimed the spider, in a lilting island accent.

Dylan did a double take. "I can't believe *you* can talk!"

"Course I talk, mon. Spiders the greatest storytellers in Xamaica!"

"So this is Xamaica!"

"Of course, mon! Are you from Babylon?"

"Where's Babylon?"

"Chuh—if you have to ask, you living in Babylon and don't even know it. Truth."

"Why did you tie up my friends?"

"I'm not trying to do no hurty-hurt. I'm saving them!"

"For dinner?"

"No, mon, me don't eat humans for dinner. Dem more for dessert!"

Alarm bells went off in Dylan's head. "Did you do anything with my sister?"

"Dat was a joke, mon! You're the first humans I've seen!"

Ines and Eli had escaped the web and were now by Dylan's side.

"You're free!" the spider exclaimed. He sounded distraught. "I and I a spider who cannot spin a web. I can't even tie my shoes!"

The spider began to cry, huge tears flowing out of all eight eyes. If the creature hadn't been so terrifying, it might have been pitiful.

"Who are you?" Dylan asked.

"Nestuh of Akbeth Akbar," it sobbed. "I and I am the youngest of 1,555 children."

"Hey, look at this!" Eli was twirling around in his wheelchair. He pulled a wheelie, rolled straight up a tree, and did a back flip.

Nestuh's mood brightened a bit. "It is the power of a spider's web. There is magic in it. It is a reflection of the magic of the Great Web of the World."

"You mean the giant web across the sky?" Dylan asked. "What's the deal with that?"

If spiders could smile, it certainly appeared that Nestuh

was doing so. He sat down and crossed six of his eight legs. "When we tell a story in Xamaica, we always start and end this way. We say, *Krik krak, Nanni's back.*"

"Why?" Dylan said.

"To put a hex on Nanni's evil ears! Am I telling this story or you? See, before the beginning, there was Jah, the orishas, and music."

"What are orishas?" Dylan asked.

"The forever spirits!" Nestuh declared. "See, Jah formed the world—he make sea into mountain, and beasts into birds. But every orisha took shape based on tings dem sing—the Rolling Calves, the Iron Lions. But two creatures, dem have no song: the spider—and Nanni."

"Nanni?" asked Dylan.

"She the greatest of witches," Nestuh answered. "She try to stop the music—"

"I don't get this," Ines cut in. "We should be running or looking for a giant can of bug spray. Why are we sitting here listening to a story?"

Out of a waist-pouch, Nestuh removed a long pipe. He put it to his lips and puffed. Bubbles floated out. He waited for Ines to stop talking.

"I thought you liked stories and adventures and all that crap," Eli said to Ines. "I mean, that's what your stupid TV show is about anyway."

"You're such a hater! You don't know anything about me or my show!"

"Quiet!" Dylan snapped. "I'm listening to Nestuh!"

"The spider went to the forest to make a drum," Nestuh continued, as if he had never been interrupted. "He pounded out a beat. He mixed pieces of all the shattered songs. The beasts followed his riddim and made music that was even greater than before."

"So what happened *after* the spider beat the drum?" Dylan asked.

"Jah came down to check what was going on. The spider hid in his drum. But Jah smiled and tapped on the drum eight times . . ."

"And the spider grew eight legs," Eli said.

"Jah whispered: *I name you Anancy, god of all spiders. Spin your web and unite all creatures. Liberty, Equality, Vitality, and Mystery shall hold your web at the four corners of Xamaica— until world's end.*"

"Krik krak," Dylan finished. "Nanni's back."

"You pick it up quickly," Nestuh said. "The most important thing about storytelling is knowing when it's the end! There's another tale about Ma Sinéad, the pirate queen who sails the skies, unshatters the shattered—"

Dylan broke in: "Enough stories. Are you sure you didn't see a little girl come by here a few minutes before us?"

The forest all around them suddenly began to shake with the sound of an enormous voice that was louder than rock concerts, airplanes, and building demolitions combined. The ground rumbled and branches tumbled from trees. The children covered their ears with their hands and still couldn't keep the noise out.

"Nectar is *dripping,* so let's get to *sipping!*" the voice announced.

"What in the world was that?" Eli asked.

But Nestuh was gone. All that was left were a few bubbles.

Two hummingbirds were hovering in the air in front of the children. They were bigger than normal hummingbirds—about the size of a Thanksgiving turkey. Each one was wearing a leather vest with an emblem of a golden crown with wings on the right breast and, in the center of the uniform, a glowing gold number. The number was different for each bird, and every few seconds each figure would shift, moving up or down a few places, from, say, 190 to 210 or 1,600 to 1,578.

"Look at them!" Ines said, pointing at the birds. "I used to be something of an ornithophobe—but these birds are just the cutest!"

Eli tapped her shoulder and pointed to the sky.

Hundreds of hummingbirds fluttered overhead—they looked like an army.

"I thought they were cute," Ines groaned. "Now, not so much."

The hummingbirds hovered lower, their swords glinting in the sunlight.

CHAPTER TEN

"This is a restricted area," chirped a hummingbird with a patch over one eye and the number 757 on his chest. "You'll need to pay one hundred wishcoins—each."

"Is a wishcoin like money?" Dylan asked.

One hummingbird with the number 182 on his chest and a voice gruffer than any hummingbird had a right to have guffawed. "They're much more than money. Wishcoins are how anyone pays for anything around here. Collect a million of 'em and they're good for one wish from the Iron Lions."

"A million? That sounds like a lot," Eli said.

"Not for birds," the patch-eyed hummingbird twittered.

"Why are you guys so rich?" Eli asked.

"We manage everyone's wishcoins," the gruff-voiced bird declared.

"So you get paid the most because you hold on to everyone else's pay?" Eli said.

"We take all the risks," the patch-eyed bird explained. "It's only fair."

"What kind of risks are you taking?" Eli asked.

"Gambling, of course," the gruff-voiced bird chirped. "What else would intelligent creatures do with their riches?"

Eli looked incredulous. "What happens when you lose?"

"Why, then we have a wishcoin support program. The whole kingdom contributes. It wouldn't be right for the creatures who are taking all the risks not to have a safety net."

Eli shook his head. "So if the kingdom gives you a safety net, shouldn't you share the wealth?"

The two birds looked at each other.

"If I weren't paid enormous sums for what I do," the gruff-voiced bird huffed, "why would I even get out of my tree in the morning?"

"The long day is *breaking,* so my bath I am *taking,*" said the ridiculously loud voice from before.

Dylan and his friends covered their ears, their skulls throbbing with the sound, but the birds didn't even blink. Dylan wondered if birds *could* blink. He should have paid more attention to the Professor's lectures.

Ines moaned: "That voice is annoying!"

The two birds both shook their heads. "They don't know about the Grand Chirp," the gruff-voiced bird squawked.

"The Grand Chirp?" Eli asked. "That's a thing?"

"How else would we know what Baron Zonip is doing?" the gruff-voiced bird replied. Just then, its number fell from 182 to 2,896, and the patch-eyed bird's rose from 757 to 500. "Kiss my tail feathers!" the gruff one cursed.

"What do those numbers mean?" asked Dylan.

"The Baron ranks every bird in the kingdom," the bird explained.

"Based on what?" Eli asked.

"Two things: Whatever He Thinks and None of Your Business."

"Something tells me they're not from this branch of the world," the patch-eyed hummingbird chirped suspiciously. "We'd better take them in."

The birds marched them away.

Dylan found it fascinating to see birds marching, particularly hummingbirds, who aren't naturally given to flying in formation, much less belonging to military organizations. On the ground, soldiers march in straight lines. How pedestrian of them. In the air, the hummingbird brigade flew in ever-changing three-dimensional geometric patterns—shifting spheres, rotating cubes, spinning pyramids. The effect was kaleidoscopic and mesmerizing and would have also been entertaining had Dylan not been the center of this flying formation, held as an unwilling, unflying, unhappy prisoner.

Dozens of the birds had grabbed hold of each of them and carried them aloft like laundry on a line. In the video game, areas of Xamaica were separated by levels and players could only visit a small region of the island. Now Dylan could see for miles. He, Eli, and Ines swept past the waterfalls, a veil of golden mist against the green face of the hills. They were traveling along the coast, where the crimson clay of the land met the blue of the sea. With all this space, Dylan wondered, how would he ever find his little sister? What was the line Emma had quoted? *Everything you can imagine is real.* Dylan began to think that maybe this *was* all real in some way. If he could just get his powers back—even a bit of them—he could find clues about Emma.

"When we play Xamaica back on Earth, we only get to travel in the gray lands," said Eli, who was being carried, wheelchair, laptop, and all, by a squadron of hummingbirds. "I think they're over there—shrouded by mist with the Moongazers all round."

Dylan looked down. "You can see creatures disappearing and reappearing in the mists! I'm guessing that when you play the game, your avatar appears in this world. When you log out, it blinks back out."

"So where are our avatars?" Eli asked.

"No clue. I could sure use the Duppy Defender right now."

"Do they have any air sickness bags on this flight?" Ines groaned. "I'm gonna hurl."

Eli laughed. "I'll never watch your show the same way again. Not that I was watching it much before." He tapped the helmet of the patch-eyed bird—one of the many hummingbirds carrying him. "Can't you go faster? And can we get a closer look at some of the territory down there?"

Big mistake.

The birds all went into a steep dive, and Dylan felt like he was heading down the craziest roller coaster ever. He tried to stay focused on the land below. The game Xamaica clearly didn't impact the real Xamaica, except along the fringes. Playing Xamaica the game was like visiting Ellis Island without seeing Manhattan—it was just an entry point into something bigger and more sweeping. Dylan hadn't seen any of the avatars of the kids he had met while playing the game. But none of them had reached beyond the forty-third level. The time he had managed to inch onto the forty-fourth level and carve his initial into the palm tree was the only mark he had ever left on Xamaica. He was in totally unmapped territory, and somehow, someway, he had to find his sister.

Ines had squeezed her eyes shut. "Tell them to stop!"

Eli was scared too but tried to play it cool. "Who is this Baron Zonip they're tweeting about?" he asked Dylan. "Is he their leader or something?"

Dylan started chewing his fingernails. "I just hope he knows where my sister is."

Building speed, the procession passed over a field of flowers. Giant bees in tan uniforms—workers?—flitted below. The flowers were massive, the size of lampposts. The smell was amazing—like breathing sunlight. Soon, a mighty forest of trees appeared in the distance. The physics of this world were different—things could obviously grow taller, wider, and brighter. The forest was made up of palm trees, but they were the size of skyscrapers. And above, over the fronds, a small city was constructed. There were buildings and passageways, storefronts and houses, all balanced on branches by some incredible architectural skill or magic. And above all floated a vast green cloud, full and fluffy as a mattress stuffed with money.

"Ssithen Ssille—the legendary hummingbird kingdom!" Eli shouted. "In the game, I thought this place was just a rumor!"

Now the brigade of birds was flying in dizzying loops trying to intimidate their involuntary guests. But Dylan stayed focused on what he was seeing. Ssithen Ssille was magnificent, astounding, and all those adjectives and phrases people generally pull out when they see the Grand Canyon for the first time, or Mount Rushmore or the Taj Mahal. Dylan felt like he was seeing all of those places together, with the Empire State Building and the Great Wall of China thrown in for good measure. The view before him was the Seven Wonders of the World—squared.

They overheard the warrior birds chirping some basic information about the city, but the sights spoke for themselves. In fact, they shouted for themselves, and the words echoed in the wind. Before them was the Golden Grove, a stand of mahoe trees with silver trunks, platinum branches, and golden leaves. Each tree was the size of a city block, maybe bigger, and all were made of a magical alloy that kept them supple and gloriously alive as they swayed gently in the wind. The children were told that each tree belonged to a particular hummingbird clan, and they were handed down from generation to generation. Dylan could see whole communities of birds tucked away in the shining branches—buildings and baths and porches and all the kinds of things you might see in gated communities and exclusive neighborhoods back on Earth. This was the ultimate high society. Dylan had never seen a forest like this one.

"Talk about your family trees," Eli said.

They were now zooming into the heart of the Golden Grove. Ines's hair was flapping in the wind, and Eli was clutching at his glasses to keep them from flying off. On the tops of seven trees clustered together was a grouping of massive nests. In each nest were eggs—not just a couple eggs, not just a dozen, but possibly thousands, all of them green with yellow spots, and arranged in intricate fragile piles. Storks dressed in sterile-looking white uniforms—Dylan figured they were doctor birds—hovered around the eggs. There was a commotion atop one of the trees and several of the doctor birds fluttered closer. As the brigade turned away, Dylan caught a glimpse of a baby hummingbird emerging from its shell.

The hummingbird city stretched on for more than a mile. At the center of the vast urban grove was a towering tornado. The twister spun and raged but remained in a single spot, surrounded by a swirl of branches, leaves, and dust. At the top of this tower of wind was a castle fortress—the structure was motionless, but it was encircled by a barrier that spun around like a roulette wheel. In fact, the wall seemed to be a massive game of chance—there were chicken scratch–like markings along its sides that may have been numbers, and a big golden egg tumbled on top of the enclosure as it spun, coming to rest, from time to time, in one spot or another.

At such moments there would be a surge of bird wails accompanied by a matching number of delighted twitters, and the birds soaring in the air or perched in the branches would settle their bets, or so Dylan guessed, since whatever currency they were exchanging was invisible to his eyes.

The birds flew their prisoner-guests over the spinning barricade, under a huge arch adorned with giant stone birds with outstretched wings on either side, and then through a glittering white passageway, before landing in a high-ceilinged, gem-encrusted room. There, the birds let Dylan, Eli, and Ines stumble to their feet. With his one good eye, the patch-eyed hummingbird winked and flitted away.

Ines flicked her hair back into place. "They didn't even give us an in-flight snack."

They glanced around. In the center of the room was a globe filled with huge worms.

"Welcome, *guests*, to my humble *nest*," said a voice, louder than all thunder.

There, at the end of the great chamber, was a hummingbird. It reminded Dylan of the time he went with the Professor and Emma to visit the Lincoln Memorial in Washington, DC. This hummingbird, like that famous Lincoln statue, dominated the room, filled it up, suffused the walls with his presence. It was clearly the master of all things with wings. It radiated wisdom and benevolence and made Dylan wonder if the term *birdbrain* was more of a compliment than an insult.

The great bird had to be Baron Zonip.

This most regal of hummingbirds had a throne that was a nest made of gold leaves. It didn't seem comfortable, but it certainly looked expensive. On the left side of the bird king was something that appeared to be a silver seashell. The bird king had just been speaking into it, so Dylan reasoned that it must be what the bird used to broadcast the Grand Chirp. On the right side of it was a huge drum, several times larger than Dylan, decorated with pictures of spiders. Was it a gift from some delegation of arachnids? Or the spoils of war?

This is bird-watching heaven, Dylan thought. *The Professor would love this.*

The scratches on his chest throbbed. He tried to ignore the pain.

All around the room were murals depicting the hummingbird king and his heroic adventures—helping chicks under attack, defeating evildoers, and saving Xamaica (and countless eggs) repeatedly. There was also a gilded mosaic celebrating the work of the hummingbird nation. It showed various creatures giving treasures to the birds to count and store. The birds took in real valuables and handed out tokens—Dylan figured they were wishcoins. In every picture, the hummingbird's nests, buildings, and palaces were filled with stacks of the glittering coins.

On either side of the Baron stood two guards, beaks tipped with serrated silver blades. On a small stand near his throne were stacked some dog-eared books. Dylan quickly scanned the titles: *Thus Chirped Zarathustra, The Invisible Talon: Avian Economic Theory,* and *To Kill a Mockingbird: Modern Methods of Capital Punishment.*

But the children's eyes were captivated not by the books or the murals or the guards, but by the Baron himself. There was something innately elegant about his movements; he had an undeniable imperial quality. His plumage was black, yellow, and green, and he had swooshing tail feathers that were longer than the rest of his body. He wore a black coat that almost looked like a tuxedo jacket with tails. His broad red chest was crisscrossed with two black sashes. Balanced on his beak was a pair of ink-black circular glasses. And on his head, he wore a top hat with a glowing gold number in the middle: *1*.

The kids stood before the Baron of Birds, the King of Clouds, the Emperor of Air.

CHAPTER ELEVEN

The Baron was every inch a monarch—though there weren't that many inches to him.

Although some of the other hummingbirds were relatively huge as far as hummingbirds go, the Baron, ruler of them all, was not a big bird. He wasn't even a medium-sized one. In fact, he was even smaller than a normal Earth hummingbird, which is to say a little shorter than this sentence.

At first, Dylan was taken aback by the king's small stature. But then again, Napoleon was short. So were Alexander the Great, John Adams, James Madison, 99 percent of all movie stars, and 100 percent of Gandhi. So why not a teeny-weenie bird baron?

"Let me do the talking," Ines said to the others. "On my show, I've met three presidents and two popes. Or is that a pair of presidents and three popes? All I remember is two of them were wearing funny hats."

The Baron spoke into his seashell: "I *think* I am giving my guests a *drink*."

The children tried in vain to cover their ears. The Grand Chirp was even louder when you were this close to the Grand Chirper. "You don't have to use that, we're standing right here!" Eli yelped.

"I know, right?" Ines moaned, rubbing her ears.

"I am Baron Zonip!" the Baron declared. His voice—sans the seashell—was a tiny tweet. Dylan had to bend forward and cup a hand to his ear just to hear it.

With that, the Baron grandly motioned to his court, and Dylan, Ines, and Eli were each handed a long-stemmed flower. The bulb of each was filled with an emerald liquid substance the consistency of syrup.

"I think we're supposed to drink this," Dylan said.

Eli stuck out his tongue. "Gross!"

"I had to eat a lot worse when I filmed an episode in Libya," Ines said. "Trust me, camel brain doesn't go down easy. Bottoms up!"

She raised her flower to drink and Dylan and Eli did the same.

"It's some kind of nectar," Eli said, licking his lips. "It's like the best soda crossed with the greatest sports drink ever!"

"No, it's more than that—it's something magical!" Dylan said.

An almost impossibly happy vision filled Dylan's mind as if it were happening to him right then and there. He was a young Iron Lion and he was flying for the first time. Feeling the wind against his wings was a thrilling joy—like his whole body was smiling.

"I'm feeling it too," Ines said. "In my mind, I'm a Wata Mama in a clear cool stream."

"I'm a Steel Donkey, eating my first bucket of iron oats," Eli added. "The nectar—it's like liquid memories."

The Baron laughed with glee as he saw the children enjoying the nectar. And if you've never heard a bird laugh—it's a breezily charming sound, almost like wind chimes, and it's hard not to smile along. "We call the drink Sslinder Sslee," he chirped. "We milk it from the Green Cloud."

"I think we saw the Green Cloud! Where does it come from?" Ines asked.

"Let's just call it our intellectual property!" the Baron laughed.

The Baron's helpers brought more flowers to drink. The refreshments were surprisingly filling—the kids soon felt stuffed, and their heads were spinning with magic memories. After a polite pause, the Baron motioned for them to introduce themselves.

"I'm Dylan."

"I'm Eli."

"And I'm Ines Mee. My name was the twenty-seventh most searched-for term on the web last year."

Eli shook his head. "I don't think he needs to know that."

"I have many fans on the Net," Ines huffed. "I won't apologize for it."

"Tell me: are you from Babylon?" the Baron inquired.

"People keep asking that," Dylan said. "What's Babylon?"

"A place of illusion—of fossil fuels and supermodels, of plastic surgery and paper money."

"You say it like those are bad things," Ines grumbled.

"If Babylon is what you call Earth, yeah, we're from there," Dylan said.

Eli raised a fist. "Brooklyn in the house!"

"You're from New Rock just like me!" Dylan whispered to Eli.

"The bird doesn't know that," Eli whispered back. "I'm just trying to get us some street cred!"

"What are you doing in Xamaica?" the Baron asked.

"I'm searching for my sister—her name is Emma," Dylan explained. "She's a human girl, about yaaaaaay high, with braids. She likes to quote people that nobody's heard of who probably died thousands of years ago anyway. Have you seen her?"

"You are the first humans we've seen in many moons. But I will spread the word among my people to keep watch for this . . . Emma."

Dylan wanted to ask the Baron how he could trigger his powers and why the cheat code wasn't working. But Ines and Eli didn't know about the code, and something told Dylan he shouldn't go telling every creature he met that he was powerless.

"Well, there's something else we're looking for," Ines broke in. "We're looking for the Root of Xamaica."

"What?" Eli blurted, spitting out his nectar in surprise.

"Since when?" Dylan asked.

Ines reached into her backpack and pulled out something she had folded inside: a huge crimson feather. Dylan could feel the magic coming off the feather like heat from a stove. He touched it with a finger and for a second he felt lighter than air; he noticed that as she gripped it, Ines's feet were hovering a few inches from the ground.

"This feather is connected to what I'm looking for," Ines said.

"What's all this about?" Eli asked.

A clucking, tweeting, and even a little quacking erupted among the members of the hummingbird court; all beaks were turned toward the huge feather, which was longer than any bird in the room by far.

"So the prophecy is true," the Baron mused. "There is but one who could have conjured such a feather: Nanni, Queen of the Dark Interval, Mistress of the Maruunz, Sorceress of the Land of Look Behind!"

There was much more clucking and tweeting from the court, and, from some of the more excited members, a little honking, hooting, and gobbling.

The Baron told the kids that after the end of the Great Music, Queen Nanni had complained to Jah that she had been given no song. Jah told her that she had been granted the greatest gift of all: silence, the dark interval between the notes, without which there is no music. Ashamed nonetheless, she had fled into the Land of Look Behind, clearing a path with a machete of fire. The other creatures of Xamaica laughed and pointed at her retreating backside and said, *Krik krak, Nanni's back!*

Angered, ever afterward Nanni had terrorized Xamaica, the Baron explained. Under cover of darkness, her minions staged acts of destruction. They were untrackable, and seemed to blend in with the night. They called themselves the Confederacy of Shadows.

"What does any of this have to do with the feather?" Ines asked.

"There is no creature that flies today with such plumage. In Time Out of Mind, perhaps, but not now. The feather could be the product of one of Nanni's evil spells."

"Nanni's an enchantress, right?" Eli said. "Doesn't she have some sort of magic book with all the wealth of the world between its covers? Not saying we want it or anything."

"Nanni is an evil witch. Her ill-gotten goods are none of our concern. We are a peaceful people. Our greatest concerns are our flowers and our eggs—and the principles under which we—"

"Okay, this is all great, but I kinda need to find Emma," Dylan interrupted. "Can I borrow the Grand Chirper thing?"

The huge hall fell silent. There was not a peep. There was a squishy plop of something the Baron's birdbath cleaners would have to deal with later.

"There are rules to using the Grand Chirper," declared the Baron. "Every chirp must rhyme. A subject can only be chirped about the same way once. And the chirp must be shorter than thirteen words or the sonic blast could shake the kingdom."

"I'll take that as a yes," Dylan said.

He marched up to the Grand Chirper and put the silver shell to his mouth. Feedback echoed through Ssithen Ssille.

This time it was the Baron and the other birds who had to cover their ears—or whatever it is that birds have under their feathers.

What to say? And what rhymed with his sister's name?

"Come back soon, little *Emma*," Dylan began. "Or big brother will be in a *dilemma*."

The booming chirp echoed through the hall. Eli and Ines, who now covered their ears too, shook their heads.

"That's the best rhyme you got?" Eli groaned. "You need to listen to more rap."

The Baron took the silver seashell back from Dylan and handed it to an underling, who quickly wiped it with a damp rag before putting it back on its stand.

"Enough of such things," the Baron announced. "You will all be my guests for the night and, in the morning, I will hold a feast in your honor!"

Dylan and his friends talked to the Baron for hours. Xamaica, they learned, was an island of roughly the same size as Jamaica—they were interdimensional twins of a sort. Beyond the island, the rest of this planet appeared to be water.

The island was ruled by several great powers. Ssithen Ssille, the hummingbird kingdom, dominated the North. Akbeth Akbar, the society of spiders, prevailed in the South. Wholandra, the pyramid city of the Iron Lions, was in the East, and Si-Ling, the empire of the Rolling Calves, was in the West. The waters around the island were run by Ma Sinéad, the pirate queen. All sorts of creatures lived in the center of the island, but the most feared figure was Nanni, who answered to no one and lived in the shadowy reaches of the Land of Look Behind, beyond the Black River, deep in the Blue Mountains. All the powers in Xamaica were in an uneasy truce, but Nanni's attacks threatened its stability. The Baron said he was doing his best to uphold the principles of the Great Web and to prevent hostilities from escalating. He just needed the other kingdoms to grant him more powers, and put more soldiers under his command, so he could finally finish Nanni.

"We hummingbirds do the most critical work on the island—counting the wishcoins," the Baron told them. "Nanni's actions threaten some of our servants—physicians, craftsmen, artists, and the like. They're nonessential workers, but it is my firm belief that all should be protected. Nanni must be stopped."

"Maybe this is beside the point, but I don't get why counting wishcoins is so important," Dylan said.

"Of course you don't," the Baron guffawed. "If I were to really explain it to you—and I wouldn't do that—the explanation would be so complex, so profound, that your eyes would melt, your ears would bleed, and your heart would likely stop."

"Seriously?" Dylan said.

"From across the worlds, through magic screens, I have studied your financial news networks, your Wall Street zillionaires, your hip-hop stars. I learned all I know about money from them."

Eli looked skeptical. "In the murals you have around here, there are piles of wishcoins. How come I don't see any in the palace?"

"My boy, of course they're here. The Golden Grove is stuffed with wishcoins! Look harder! Look deeper! Look smarter!"

Eli tried, and so did Ines; Dylan stared until his head hurt and his eyebrows felt hot.

"I think I see a little glittering in the corner . . ." Ines began.

"I'm not getting anything," Dylan admitted. "Wait, maybe I see a stack of something by the throne . . . No, still nothing . . ."

The palace erupted with the wind-chimey laughter of the birds. "It seems that your human minds cannot handle the intricacies of economics," the Baron chortled. "It truly takes a birdbrain to understand how our financial system works!"

"But why do you need so much money?" Eli asked.

Dylan had never seen a bird smirk before, but the Baron did exactly that, which is a tough thing to pull off if you've got a beak. "It is the poor that make the rich," the Baron tweeted. "Money is just metal or paper or dreams unless everyone agrees it is something more. If you look in the mirror and see a worm, why blame the bird that eats you?"

"I thought hummingbirds only eat nectar," Eli said.

The Baron smiled again, and summoned his warrior birds. "I'm going to give you all the hospitality my kingdom can offer. There are many spies about, traitors, agents of Nanni. But I get a good feeling from you. I hope you reward my trust . . . The night winds are *blowing*," he blurted into the Grand Chirper. "And my guests must be *going*."

So Dylan and his friends were once again borne aloft by birds.

"This place is like a mirror image of Jamaica," Dylan remarked to the other kids as they flew. "I mean, except for the talking birds and the evil sorceress and everything. What's up with that? Why Jamaica?"

"What is the Caribbean?" Eli offered. "It's where the old world meets the new. It makes sense that other worlds would intersect there too."

Dylan looked down and saw various Xamaican creatures—Rolling Calves, Iron Lions, even dragons—hard at work in the hummingbird kingdom. They were plowing fields, constructing buildings, pulling vast stores of goods stacked on carts.

Meanwhile, above the trees, hummingbirds lived in leisure, zipping through the Green Cloud, flitting about the flowers, and tweeting tunes. Now and again, a drop of nectar would trickle down a tree trunk or a leaf and the beasts on the ground would push and shove one another to get in a position to catch it on their tongue.

"Seems like the creatures on the ground work pretty hard to support the folks up here," Dylan said to the patch-eyed hummingbird.

"Don't look down," the bird responded, in a voice mean enough to scramble eggs. The number on its chest had fallen from 500 to 15,562.

Dylan realized he had no idea where these birds were taking them.

CHAPTER TWELVE

The soldier birds put the kids in guest accommodations in a tall palm tree. A large nest made of sticks and mortar had been built at the top, complete with a minibar of sorts stocked with coconuts filled with the nectar drink that the Baron had given them before.

"This tree was grown from the seeds of the great Palm of Protection," a soldier bird declared. "Nanni grew the first palm when she hid in the wilderness, so no one could find her unless she wanted to be found. Nothing may harm you while you rest among its fronds."

Then the birds flew away.

"Best. View. Ever." Ines said, surveying the forest. "Reminds me of the time I rented the Eiffel Tower for my eleventh birthday party. Except for the Parisians mobs cursing me in French, of course."

"Yo, we have to talk," Dylan said to her. "If I'm gonna find Emma, I need to know everything. That huge feather you pulled out—I've seen that before."

"No way—it's one of a kind," Ines replied.

But a six-foot red feather wasn't something that Dylan would just forget. Well, he had, but now it was another memory that had surfaced. He had images in his head of many huge crimson feathers, and a plane—and a beastly roar. But he couldn't quite sort out if he was recalling a nightmare, something real, or something in between.

"What other magic stuff do you have in that bag of tricks?" Dylan asked.

"Probably plenty," Eli chimed in, then turned his laptop around so Dylan could see the screen.

"You can get a connection here?" Dylan shook his head in admiration. Back in the real world, Dylan never really saw Eli play Xamaica, but he did see him spend a crazy amount of time trying to steal its secrets. That was how Dylan had first gotten the cheat code. Eli had been looking for passwords that could get him past Xamaica's firewalls. Dylan had just been playing around with what Eli had already done and stumbled across the most potent password of all—the ultimate cheat code. All he had to do was say it, and he was the most powerful avatar around. If only it worked now.

"Take a look," Eli said.

Xamaicapedia:
The Gamer's Guide to Saving the World
A publication of Fiercely Independent Booksellers Inc.
(A wholly owned subsidiary of Mee Corp. Enterprises.)

I-Got-Your-Back Pack: a magic shoulder sack the size of a regular backpack with unlimited room inside. Extremely useful for transporting helpful things on dangerous quests. It can carry weapons, carry food, and carry a tune; it can also hold your horses, hold your temper, and hold onto your hats. Under no circumstances, however, should you use it to hold someone's feet to the fire—like many Mee Corp. products, the pack is extremely flammable.

"So I have a few things," Ines huffed. "A girl has to be prepared."

"You're full of surprises," Dylan said.

"She's full of something," Eli agreed. "What was that about the Root of Xamaica? That's not even in the *Xamaicapedia.*"

"It's why I came to Xamaica—I need the Root for something, let's just leave it at that," Ines said. "Why did you ask about Nanni's book?"

"The only reason I entered your stupid tournament was for the Grand Major Triple-Secret Prize," Eli fumed. "I have to get something out of this. I want to find that book!"

"I would trade that book, *and* her freakish feather, to get my sister back so we can get out of here," Dylan added. "Do you think the birds have her?"

"If they were capturing people, why'd they let us go?" Eli asked.

Dylan shook his head. "We're not exactly free."

"You're right—we're five hundred feet up," Ines said. "How are we going to get down? And, more importantly, is there room service?"

Just then, an explosion lit up the night. The blast came from the direction of the seven nest-egg trees. Flames leapt up to the sky, squawking filled the air, and the world shook.

"A Rolling Calf stampede!" Eli shouted. "That crack was one running into a trunk. But normally they would never charge into a forest, so someone must have steered them here."

"But why?" Dylan said.

"There's a saying—*Only death stops a Rolling Calf stampede.* Whoever did this . . ."

"Must want to kill somebody," Dylan finished.

Another loud crack—a nearby tree shuddered and began to topple as, presumably, a Rolling Calf struck it from below. Other trees were falling too. Dylan could smell smoke— the forest was on fire and their tree was burning. Dylan whispered his cheat code to himself two times. Nothing.

"You want to tell me what you're doing?" Eli inquired.

"Nope," Dylan responded, his face feeling hot, and not just from the flames.

The kids heard a voice calling them through the flickering shadows: "Jump!" Nestuh was at the bottom of the tree trunk and had spun a web to catch their fall.

"That's the worst web I ever saw," Eli whined. "That's not gonna break our fall. It's gonna break our backs."

"Trust me, mon!" Nestuh shouted up. "Jump!"

"Hello? I don't have working legs!"

"I got eight arms, mon!" Nestuh said. "To me, you all look like you missing limbs!"

The flames were shooting from below, racing up the tree trunk, even as the kids spotted a squadron of warrior birds flying toward them.

"We should wait for the birds to help," Ines advised.

"They may be coming to finish us off!" Eli warned.

"You heard what they said—we can't come to harm in the Palm of Protection," Ines said. "The stampede is down there. We should stay up here."

"But what if the palm burns down?" Eli asked.

The flames had reached the top of the tree. "Ines—think of something!" Dylan urged. "Do what you do on your show! Turn a hangnail into a hang glider or something!"

Ines looked at the flames, and then she lay down and curled up like a baby.

"Did I miss that episode?" Eli asked.

Dylan chewed on his fingernails. "She's bailing on us!"

The flames were reaching higher and it was getting hotter and smokier. Dylan peered around—he had to think his way out of this situation. He grabbed a handful of the feathers that lined the nest. "If only we could fly!"

"That's it!" Eli declared. "I have a plan! We need her I-Got-Your-Back Pack!"

Ines emerged from her stupor. "Why? Oh—I get it!"

She took out the crimson feather and all three kids grabbed hold.

Dylan and Ines jumped off the nest, with Eli rolling beside them. They hurtled through the dark holding the feather and each other. Dylan felt a magical tingling as the feather began breaking their fall. The three kids were floating gently to the earth while flames and sparks jumped up all around.

"Uh-oh," Ines breathed.

The edges of the feather had caught fire, and the kids had to let it go. They were falling again, and fast—this was going to hurt. They hit the ground hard, right next to the worst-spun web they had ever seen.

"Ow!" Dylan moaned.

"Urh!" Eli grunted.

"Ouch!" Ines yelped.

The ashes of the crimson feather fell like black snowflakes all around them. Nestuh was crying again. "I and I a failure! I can't even spin a web right!"

"At least we're alive," Ines said, rubbing her back. "I think."

"Nobody thinks I can do anything right!" sobbed the spider. "I'm the youngest of 1,555 kids. They're all sisters— my father wanted a boy. After that kind of buildup, of course I was a disappointment. My mother ate him soon after I was born."

"Don't tell me—you're a black widow," Dylan said.

"From a long line of black widows, mon. And unless I prove myself in the world, my sisters swear I'll be the next family meal."

"I'd love to hear about your family problems, but we have to get out of here," Eli interjected.

He pointed at the sky. The warrior birds were circling the tree. It was only a matter of time before they spotted the kids.

"The Rolling Calves are that way," Nestuh said.

"Then we need to go the other way," Eli responded.

They all started to run. Well, actually, Dylan and Ines ran, Eli pulled himself back into his wheelchair and kinda floated and rolled, and Nestuh did that crawling and scampering thing that arachnids do. Above them, it seemed as if the whole treetop city was in an uproar. Dylan saw more soldier birds flying toward the conflagration. Doctor birds, some carrying chicks, others carrying cracked eggs, flew away from it. Something like a wail went up—a mournful, horrible sound that Dylan immediately wished he hadn't heard and prayed that he would never have to listen to ever again.

Dylan also wished he hadn't seen the awful ruin of the nest trees. It was a horrifying vision. Flames twirled on the tops of the trees like angry ballet dancers. Branches broke and fell off all afire. Egg white dripped from the upper reaches in sad, goopy strands. Long stretches of golden yolk sagged down from the palm fronds. Pieces of eggshells tumbled through the air to the ground. The disaster was made all the more horrendous by something that the Baron had told Dylan. Hummingbirds mate once, and for life. The mothers lay a single egg, which is then incubated for ten years. They can never lay another. As the fire raged, Dylan could only think of the loss of all those dreams, all those hopes, all up in smoke.

Dylan saw something else he wished he hadn't seen: the patch-eyed hummingbird, tears streaming out of his one good eye, flying back toward the fires. It happened in a flash, but it was so awful, his mind held the image, like a photo.

It was then that the children heard the Grand Chirp.

"FOREVER SHALL THIS NIGHT BE INFAMOUS! THE BABYLONIANS HAVE REPAID KINDNESS WITH BETRAYAL! DEATH TO THEM, AND THEIR QUEEN NANNI! TO ARMS! WE MUST RESTORE OUR ANCIENT POWERS! WE MUST DEFEND XAMAICA FROM NANNI'S CONFEDERACY OF SHADOWS!"

"He just broke every Grand Chiper rule!" Eli yowled. "And my eardrums!"

"Queen Nanni set us up!" Ines said. "Now the King thinks we're part of her awful Confederacy of Shadows!"

Over their heads, above the trees and the smoke, there was a tearing in the corner of the sky. The sound of the vast ripping was louder than a hundred lightning storms. It echoed across the clouds and shook the trees and made Dylan's bones vibrate and his teeth rattle. All the creatures of the forest answered the cacophony with howls and bellows and screams until the air was a stew of horror and dismay. Dylan covered his ears with his hands but the sound continued—on and on until dawn spilled like blood across the gray flesh of the sky. "The Groundation has begun," whispered Nestuh.

"Groundation? What does that mean?" Ines asked.

"The Great Web is falling," Nestuh said. "In three days, the crimson bird will fly again and this world will end."

CHAPTER THIRTEEN

The flames were far behind them now, but they could still smell the smoke. Given that the kids were all terrorized, tired, hungry, and scared, they were in remarkably good spirits. Part of the reason was Nestuh, who kept a positive vibration going with his general good nature, and his constant stream of stories, jokes, and comebacks. After a while, the kids were putting aside their problems and pains and chuckling along with him.

"This landscape's like a supermodel," Ines joked. "Beautiful but difficult."

"Sounds like a woman I had once," Nestuh said. "Don't

ever date a praying mantis, mon. It always ends badly."

They pushed on. Dylan would have traded all the stupid conversation and camaraderie for a clue about where his sister was. Emma and the Professor were always complaining that he couldn't stay focused and that topics started trending in his brain for a few moments and vanished just as quickly. This time, he wanted to prove them wrong and complete his search. The problem was, they weren't even looking for Emma right now, they were pretty much just fleeing. Eli was doing well enough, but he was in a wheelchair and things were getting hard for him, even with Nestuh helping to carry him. Eli motioned he was tired and that Nestuh should set him and his wheelchair down.

"Nestuh—I'm officially friending you," Eli said. "I couldn't have made it without your help."

"I know how you feel," Ines said. "This is the hardest trip I've had since the time I was mistakenly booked in coach. Trust me, you cannot get a good hot stone foot massage on a commercial flight!"

"I've got something a little more serious on my mind," Eli said. He pointed to the sky, and the huge torn corner of the Great Web. "Now what was all that about the end of the world?"

"It's the prophecy, mon," Nestuh said. "When one corner of the Great Web come down, the other three follow in three days. Truth."

"Okay, that means we got seventy-two hours to find Nanni's book," Eli said.

"You're thinking about treasure?" Ines said. "I still have

no idea where to find the Root of Xamaica! And are you forgetting about Dylan's sister?"

"You have some *cojones* ordering us around!" Eli said. "What happened to you back there?"

"What do you mean?" Ines asked.

"When it all hit the fan, you froze! I thought you were a big TV adventurer!"

"Last season you saved orphans from a mudslide," Dylan recalled.

"You rescued nuns from a burning bus during fall sweeps," Eli added.

Ines put her face in her hands and let out a loud scream. "I'm just gonna tell you: I'm not an adventurer!" she cried. "I just play one on TV!"

"What?" Dylan and Eli said together.

"It's all special effects! I'm a fraud! I'm a fake! I travel all over the world and I never get to leave my hotel room!"

Dylan spat out a sliver of fingernail. "So you've never really faced any danger?"

"Are you kidding?" Ines said. "I'm a spokesperson! You think Smokey the Bear puts out forest fires? He has people for that!"

Eli laughed loud and hard. "You asked me to believe in magic—I can't even believe in reality! My dad always says— never trust any business with more than thirty employees! You want us to go on this quest—Greatest! Adventure! Ever!—and you still haven't told us why you need this Root. Start talking, phoney!"

Dylan looked around. What would Eli say if he knew about Dylan's cheat code? Wasn't Dylan kind of a faker too?

Not that the code even worked here, but still.

Ines's dark eyes were bright and wet.

Eli snorted. "Enough with the alligator tears!"

"The right phrase is *crocodile tears,* actually," Dylan said.

"Whatever. I'm sure she's got purses made out of both. What are you crying about?"

Ines sniffed and wiped her eyes. "It's my dad. He's sick."

"Dr. Mee?" Dylan asked. "But he spoke at the tournament!"

"I get it," Eli said. "Remember I said that speech seemed old? It was a recording!"

Ines sat down on a rock and cupped her head in her hands. "I found him passed out in his study three months ago. The crimson feather was clutched in his hand. The last thing he said was, *Find the Root of Xamaica.* He hasn't spoken since. The doctors say he's in a coma, but I know it's something else—something magical. That's why I set up the tournament. That's why I followed the symbols he left behind. I knew the key was on the forty-fourth level. I needed the best players to help me. I think if I find it, I can cure my dad."

"So you need to find the Root," Dylan said. "Eli wants that book. And I have to locate my sister. How do we pull this all off?"

"Hope," Nestuh said.

"We need more than that," Eli said.

"Nah, mon. I'm talking 'bout Hope Road," Nestuh clarified. "It's the trail that runs through the island."

"Where does it lead?" Ines asked.

"It's a magic pathway. It takes you wherever you need to go."

"Can Hope Road take us to my sister?"

"It doesn't work like that. You can't pick the place—you just need to go there. And you can only use it three times. So maybe it takes you to your sister. But maybe it takes you to somewhere else you need to go first."

"So it might take me to the Root," Ines murmured.

"Or it could take me to Nanni's book," Eli added.

The kids took a vote and the result was unanimous: they would follow Hope Road. Even Nestuh raised six of his limbs in favor of the plan (he needed the other two to stand on).

"Hope Road it is then," Dylan concluded.

"How do we find it?" Ines asked.

"Once you decide to take that route," Nestuh said, "Hope Road finds you."

The children all looked down at once and saw they were on a path leading into dark woods.

Hope Road was a strange way to travel. It stretched out before Dylan and the others as far as they could see. The route was narrow and sprinkled with red rocks that glittered in the light. The whole path seemed to shimmer and shift and sway like a desert mirage.

At one point, Dylan looked back and saw, to his surprise, there was no back, and there wasn't even a *there*. The way vanished behind him as soon as he took a step forward. In back of them was only a kind of blankness. Like an empty sky after the sun sets but before the stars are out, a pencil drawing that has been erased, or something important that you just can't seem to remember.

The hike was hard. The path led over hills and through rivers. So as they walked, Nestuh told them a story to pass the time. "Krik krak, Nanni's back," the spider began.

As he spoke, he puffed on his magical pipe, one that filled the air, not with smoke, but with bubbles. In each of the bubbles, pictures appeared, images from the tale he was telling—of giant spiders, cruel witches, and misty mountains. He wove a story about the time Queen Nanni challenged Anancy to a game of Shatranj. It was a game like chess, but magical. Nanni tried to cheat—she granted her pieces temporary life and pledged that they could live on as her servants if they helped her. She taught them Bangaran, a mystical martial art of which she was the master, and her pieces became great fighters. Desperate to win, she sacrificed piece after piece in wild attacks. In this game, when pieces were captured, they really perished. They begged for mercy, but Nanni said their pain was not her problem—she only sought victory. Soon she fell into the spider's trap and was defeated. The pieces had been following her opponent's designs all along, for he had promised them freedom, which makes life worth living. Nanni had tried to ensnare Anancy in a web of deceit. But Anancy was one of those spiders who was good at untying things.

Nanni, enraged, destroyed the pieces and spread the shards over a hilly region in the Land of Look Behind. She was so full of fury she cut her hands on the fragments and her blood stained the pieces and the soil. Anancy took pity on the pieces, and gathered them up and set them on the summit of a hill. The greatest of all spiders beseeched Jah for help. The Maker of All Music, moved by the scene, breathed lasting life into each one of the chessmen, for only Jah may grant that favor, no matter Nanni's bargains.

"I name you the Maruunz," said Jah. "You will have lion hearts, and eyes the color of the Xamaican earth. You will be the most magnificent warriors Xamaica has known."

But to Nanni, he said: "Live for yourself, and you live for nothing. Yet if you give your life, you will find it. You have forced others to suffer for your ends—and now your blood will forever stain this land." That is why, Nestuh explained, Xamaican soil is a deep red, even now.

Then Jah delivered this curse to Nanni: "You will, in your long life, face a great opponent. His final victory will be your final defeat."

"Krik krak, Nanni's back," Ines said.

Eli smiled. "The most important part of storytelling is knowing when it's the end."

"So Nanni has terrorized Xamaica since then," Nestuh said, finishing his tale. "She always escapes, despite many battles and many losses. Over the centuries, she's come to terms with the spiders because we beat her fair and square. There are times when you could say we carried her on our backs. But the rest of the people of Xamaica take heart in the knowledge that a great opponent will someday defeat her."

"That's a serious curse," Eli said.

"So who is the great opponent?" Ines asked.

"Maybe it's the Game Changers," said Eli.

"Prophesies come true in unexpected ways, mon," Nestuh laughed.

"I need someone to teach me Bangaran," Dylan said.

Nestuh put away his pipe and all around the children,

the bubbles popped revealing a new landscape and the setting sun.

"I can't believe how much ground we've covered," Eli marveled.

Ines rubbed the spider on the head. "Thanks for the story. I usually travel with two producers, a camera crew, a makeup artist, a personal assistant, and a horse whisperer we keep on staff because of a union requirement. Traveling with you guys is way better—and a lot less paperwork."

"This is just the kind of adventure that Emma would have loved to tag along on," Dylan murmured. "She can be so annoying."

"Did you ever think that maybe she tagged along because she loved you?" Ines asked.

"N-n-no!" Dylan stammered.

"Of course not," Ines sighed. "Because you're a guy."

There was a gleam from over the crest of the next hill.

"Where the heck has Hope Road taken us?" Eli wondered aloud.

CHAPTER FOURTEEN

Wholandra—the city of the Iron Lions—was something to see. Actually, you couldn't see it, not all at once, not in the full glare of the afternoon. It was too big, and too bright, to absorb in one glance.

"I can't believe we're in Wholandra!" Eli said. "If we were playing the game instead of living it, we'd be racking up the adventure points!"

The children moved toward the heart of the city. Every building was a pyramid—there were small ones and large ones, structures for storage and palaces for royalty, pyramid graveyards and pyramids with swimming pools (triangular, naturally). There were pyramid restaurants and pyramid shopping centers, pyramid hospitals and even pyramid fast-food drive-thrus, which, just like their non-pyramid counterparts back on Earth, always got your order wrong, but you never realized it until you were halfway home to your own pyramid. There was also a pyramid-shaped white-collar prison.

Three pyramids towered above the others. The sides were covered in burnished bronze, inlaid with patterns of ivory and onyx, and topped with shining steel. The middle pyramid had a huge feline eye at its tippy-top, and the orb seemed to follow Dylan, unblinking. The top Iron Lions lived in this trio of buildings, according to Nestuh. When the sun hit the sides, all three pyramids lit up like stars.

"Who are you?" an Iron Lion with a red mane and golden wings asked the children as they walked down Wholane, the city's main street.

"Who are you?" Nestuh replied, and the Iron Lion nodded and flew away.

Nestuh explained: Asking "Who are you?" was just the standard way of greeting in Wholandra. Iron Lions communicated in an unusual way—that is, unusual for anyone who wasn't an Iron Lion. They only talked in questions. No statements, no declarations—only queries. This made conversation rather cryptic, and even stranger still when it was between two Iron Lions. It took awhile for anyone to get to the point.

"See, the magical power of an Iron Lion is this . . ." Nestuh began.

"I know, I know," Ines said. "If you answer its three riddles, it must grant your wish. I used to play an Iron Lion, so I'm not totally ignorant."

"That must be why Hope Road led us here," Dylan chimed in. "If we can get a wish, I can get my sister! Finally—we're making some progress!"

Dylan kept his eyes open, peeking through every triangular door and window, searching for Emma. Then the children saw the lines. Visitors from all over Xamaica had queued up outside the pyramid hoping for an audience with the Whoberatum, the Iron Lion appointed that day to ask riddles and grant wishes. There were slithery Dlos, misty Moongazers, and even a few Arrowak (half-flesh and half-plant—you had to watch out for ones that were part poison ivy).

"It's been done like this since I can remember," Nestuh said. "If the wish is small, dem questions easy. But if dem wish big, dem riddle hardy-hard."

"So what if someone asked for say—Nanni's book?" Eli asked.

"That's a hard question," Nestuh answered. "Dem get a hardy-hard riddle."

"What happens if they get the answer wrong?" Dylan asked.

"Then the Iron Lion eats them," Nestuh said. "So dem usually ask for easy wishes."

There were limits to the Iron Lions' wish-granting power, Nestuh pointed out. They couldn't do something ridiculously godlike such as bring someone back from the dead. Of course, Iron Lions never admitted to their limitations, not in public anyway. Ungrantable wishes were usually met with unanswerable riddles, like, "What's the meaning of life?"

The kids arrived at the end of the wish-granting line. There were a couple wiggly Wata Mamas, a handful of Moongazers, and a terrifying one-sided Hai-Uri, which pretty much had everyone on edge—no pun intended, though it's a good one.

"This must be how department-store Santas feel," Ines said, surveying the long line.

"Except Santa doesn't eat kids who give wrong answers," Eli said.

"What do we do now?" Dylan asked.

"Easy," Nestuh answered. "We join the line and we waity-wait."

It was a tough day for wishes. The Pharaoh of the Iron Lions himself was the Whoberatum on duty. The line was moving fast—in part because the people ahead of the kids were being steadily eaten as they failed to answer the riddles correctly.

"Have you ever seen so many beautiful wishcoins?" asked the floppy Wata Mama in line in front of the kids. They were strange creatures, these Wata Mamas. They looked like baby seals, but with human arms and faces and hair. They also tended to overshare.

"Uh, no," Dylan said.

"Just look at them!" the Wata Mama sighed. "There up ahead—millions of wishcoins in piles all around the anteroom to the pyramid!"

None of the kids saw anything. The anteroom looked

completely empty, except for the line of creatures snaking through it.

"I'm getting married in a month," the Wata Mama said. "I've worked all my life for the birds but I have nowhere near enough wishcoins for a proper wedding. This is my last chance."

"Is there any way we can help?" Eli asked. "If you get eaten, it's gonna wreck your wedding plans."

"Thanks, but I must do this," the Wata Mama replied. "You children are known among my people. Someday we'll repay your kindness."

Soon it was the Wata Mama's turn, and things weren't going well. She had answered two questions so far (barely) but was stumbling on the third one. She had asked for a sunny day for her coming marriage ceremony, which seemed like a simple request, but was actually categorized as a "major wish" because it involved moving the sun, which is tough to do, and planning a wedding, which is even harder.

"What runs but never walks, roars but never talks, has a head but never weeps, has a bed but never sleeps?" the Pharaoh had asked.

"A river!" Eli whispered to Dylan, Ines, and Nestuh. "That's easy."

The Wata Mama didn't find it so easy, even though she should have been in her element, water pun totally intended. She gave the wrong answer and the Pharaoh opened his jaws wide. He gulped the Wata Mama down tail first, so the kids could see her face as she slid down his throat. Her wide fishy eyes were only mildly surprised, as if she had been fatalistically expecting this finale all along. The Pharaoh burped after he finished devouring her, and even from three hundred feet away, the kids could smell this last meal, along with his meal before that, which happened to be a Rolling Calf. It was a two-course burp. And the kids were in danger of becoming the third.

It was their turn now. They were also the last in line; everyone in front had been eaten or left and everyone behind had lost heart. They were inside the largest pyramid, in a huge hall covered in hieroglyphics. The Pharaoh of the Iron Lions loomed before them, seated on a great stone throne. He had an extravagant golden mane, a muscular lion's body, and massive paws. His face was both human and catlike, with a broad, flat nose and long whiskers. His great black wings were folded against his sides. When he looked at the children, his gaze hit them like a jungle cat jumping on a wildebeest.

"So cool," Eli gushed. "He looks just like his action figure."

"Let me do the talking," Dylan informed his companions. "When this was just a game I was good at riddles. And it's my sister who's missing." Dylan also wanted to ask about the cheat code and why his powers weren't working, but he kept that to himself.

"I should answer the riddles," Ines declared. "It's my dad that's sick."

"I should do the talking," Eli said. "If we can answer these riddles, we can get these Iron Lions to bring us Nanni's book. That's what I came here for. To get my money."

"What's up with this money obsession?" Ines asked.

"Oh, shut up! Your family owns Mee Corp.!" Eli shot back.

"Money is not the most important thing—believe me,

I know," Ines said. "My family was just as happy when we were millionaires as when we were billionaires."

"Did you just say that? Seriously?" Eli scoffed. "You are the friggin' worst!"

"Why do you hate me so much?" Ines pouted.

"I don't hate you," Eli replied. "I hate what you stand for."

"I don't stand for anything!"

"Exactly," Eli said.

"Seriously? You're going to go there? My mom wrote music! My dad's an inventor, a businessman, and a pretty great piano player! We're makers and you're just a taker—and a hater!"

"You don't know even 1 percent of the story. This probably isn't in your files, but did you know your dad and my dad have a connection? My dad *invented* Xamaica!"

"What?" Dylan exclaimed.

"That's a lie!" Ines snapped.

"It's true!" Eli insisted. "He designed the basic software. But your dad had better lawyers. My dad did win a piece of all future games Mee Corp. put out. The joke is, you guys never put out any hit games after Xamaica. So we got nothing."

"I can't believe you're just telling me this now!" Dylan said.

"There was a confidentiality agreement—I only found this out a few weeks ago when I hacked into the Mee Corp. legal department! So that's why I hate Mee Corp. Her family is a bunch of frauds. Now I've got a chance for payback. So I want to answer the riddles!"

Suddenly all three of the kids were squabbling and shouting. Everyone was talking and nobody was listening—until a booming sound interrupted them.

"What is your wish?" the Pharaoh inquired. His words sounded like half–lion's roar, half–eagle's screech, and half–TV news anchor, which added up to more than a single voice.

"I want to find my sister," Dylan said. "I'll bargain for any clue that will help."

"Do you not realize that you are in Wholandra?" the Pharaoh boomed. "Has no one told you that all statements must be uttered in the form of questions?"

"Yes, they did—I think?" Dylan said.

"Can you state your wish now? And do you realize the consequence is death if you fail to answer my riddles?"

Ines pushed Dylan aside and stepped before the Pharaoh. "Will you grant me three wishes?" she asked in a clear voice.

The Pharaoh smiled and his teeth were like daggers.

CHAPTER FIFTEEN

The Pharaoh looked right at Ines, who was now the official wish asker.

"I may be a fraud, but I'm not selfish," she said, turning to Eli and Dylan. "I'll get a wish for each of us. Then our problems will be solved."

Dylan, Eli, and Nestuh looked at her in horror. The Pharaoh cleared his throat and spat something out which landed *plop* on the ground.

"Gross!" Eli whispered to Dylan. "Hairball."

"Do you realize that if you lose, I will eat your companions as well?" the Pharaoh asked.

"Actually, I-I-I didn't know about that part," Ines stammered. She turned to Dylan and Eli. "Do you hate me now?"

"Ask me that again in about three answers," Eli muttered.

"Then, may we begin?" the Pharaoh asked. "Question one: What goes up the stairs without moving?"

"Oh—I know this," Ines said. "Just thinking out loud here. I don't think it's anything that's really alive, that would be too easy. And it's probably something indoorsy because we're talking about stairs."

Eli started to mouth the answer but the Pharaoh shot him a look. "You do know if you help, you forfeit your lives?"

Eli zipped his lips.

Ines started dancing in a circle. "I've got it! Something that goes up stairs without moving! A rug! I mean, is it a rug?"

The Pharaoh's left eye twitched. "Question two: What gets wetter as it dries?"

"Ohh—that's another toughie," Ines muttered. "Thinking out loud again. What gets wetter while it dries? I can't think of any animal that fits that description. Hmmm. When I take a shower, I get wetter and then dry myself off. That's it! I get it now. Is it a towel?"

The Pharaoh's whole face was twitching now.

Ines smiled. "All the Iron Lion stuff from the game is coming back to me now—like riding a bike. If cats could ride bikes, that is."

Something else was coming back to her. She was looking

positively Iron Lion–like. Giant whiskers were growing on either side of her nose. Tufts of fur were suddenly sprouting on her skin. Her nails were lengthening into claws. Great gray wings were sprouting out of her back.

"Ines—you're turning into a . . ." Eli began.

"I know, I know," Ines said. "When you have a tail sprouting out of your bum, it's not the kind of thing that just slips by unnoticed."

"It's your avatar!" Dylan exclaimed. "You set off some sort of trigger!"

The Pharaoh appeared to be taken aback asking riddles to an almost–Iron Lion. Many of the other Iron Lions had come out from around the pyramid to watch. Even some of the creatures who had left the line had returned, eager to see how this contest of wills would end.

Then the Pharaoh smiled. His teeth were stained with the blood of his previous meals. There was nothing smiley about his smile. "The third and final question: Why does the man who made it not want it? Why does the man who bought it not need it? And why does the man who uses it not know?"

The Pharaoh's expression was the opposite of a Cheshire cat grin: his smile seemed to disappear, but the rest of him— his sleek muscles, his sharp claws, his piercing eyes—came into sharper focus. Ines met his gaze. A bright light shined around her, golden and shimmering, and encased her like a chrysalis. She seemed to levitate, and then the light vanished. Ines stretched her metal wings; she was completely an Iron Lion now.

The Pharaoh and Ines had a staring contest for what seemed like a week. Finally the Pharaoh blinked.

"Well, I guess this is what people usually need when they fail to answer your riddles," Ines said. "Are you talking about a coffin?"

The Pharaoh let out a roar that shook the entire pyramid.

The children and Nestuh were hustled into a back room.

Iron Lion guards, armed with sabers and shields, stood around them.

"I want my wishes!" Ines demanded. "Where is Dylan's sister? Where is the Root of Xamaica? And while you're at it, give me Nanni's book!"

The Pharaoh picked his teeth with a claw. "I ain't granting you squat."

"Wait—why didn't you say that in the form of a question?" Eli asked.

"Cut the BS," the Pharaoh spat. "There's no protocol, it's just us."

"This is *so* not cool!" Ines complained. "Why won't you give me my wishes?"

"Because I can't. There's not enough obeah. There hasn't been for years."

Magic, the Pharaoh explained, was a finite resource, and it was drying up. Magic emanated from the Great Web of the World, but Nanni was using obeah—that's what they called magic around here—with such abandon she was leaving very little for anyone else. "Her reckless harvesting of the web is what caused one corner of it to drop. If she isn't stopped, the whole web may collapse."

"But why this charade? Why the line of people asking you for wishes you can't grant?" Ines asked.

"We have to keep up appearances. We still have enough magic for the little things. Like locating lost keys, and repairing zippers. I can cast spells to fix zippers and find keys all the livelong day. But we haven't granted a major wish in a long time. Mostly we issue wishcredits."

"Yeah, we know—wishcoins," Dylan said.

"What you don't know is that wishcoins don't really exist. Way back in Time Out of Mind they did, but when the magic started fading, we figured screw it, let's just let 'em eat imagination—and people bought it. We told them wishcoins existed and they saw them, glittering in their palms. People bought houses with wishcoins, made loans with wishcoins. The whole Xamaican economy is based on them, and the hummingbirds pretend they have the most of 'em. If word ever gets out they're not real—the system will collapse."

"So basically your whole kingdom . . ." Eli started.

"Is a pyramid scheme, yes," the Pharaoh said. "We Iron Lions can't resist them. Hence the white-collar prison."

Dylan wasn't any closer to finding Emma. "So you can't send us anywhere?"

"On the contrary," the Pharaoh said.

With that, all the Iron Lions drew their sabers.

"What is this?" Ines asked, baring her teeth.

"We need magic—we're magical creatures," the Pharaoh said. "The Baron will do anything to save Xamaica from Nanni—and he thinks you're her agents. If I return you to him, he'll give me enough strands of the web to keep Wholandra operating. The sanitation in this city is magic-based—and the litter boxes haven't been changed in months."

"But everyone's using too much obeah!" Eli said. "In two days the web will fall!"

"Actually, a few prophets differ on whether web collapse is man-made, natural, or another of Queen Nanni's tricks. That's what the hummingbirds tell us."

"When real experts say the sky is falling, you should listen," Eli said.

"Why not harvest the web yourselves?" Dylan asked.

"We can't fly as high as hummingbirds. They're able to launch themselves from the tops of the trees in the Golden Grove. Plus, Queen Nanni has transformed herself into some creature from Time Out of Mind who would attack us if we tried that."

"That crimson feather . . ." Ines said.

"It must belong to this creature, whatever it is," Eli said.

So it was Queen Nanni after all. She was the crimson beast.

"It gets better," the Pharaoh continued. "The creature can steal shadows."

"So who needs a shadow?" Eli asked.

"To lose one's shadow is to be drained of dreams. It takes maybe three days before someone who loses a shadow fades away. Nanni has been recruiting freed shadows for her Confederacy of Shadows, and the Baron has been locking shadows up as fast as he can round them up. But none of this is your concern. I've got to send you back to the Baron."

"What? We're not going to be sent back," Dylan said.

"Well, then, you'll be lunch!"

The Pharaoh leapt at Dylan, but he was met in midair by Ines. The two giant felines collided and fell to the ground—both landing on all four feet, of course. And then the fight really started. In her new Iron Lion form, Ines was strong—and speedy. The Pharaoh was bigger, but less agile. The two went at it like, well, cats—clawing and biting and hissing. Ines flew all about the room before zipping out an exit with the Pharaoh in pursuit. Dylan and the others, followed by the Pharaoh's bodyguards, went out to see what would happen.

Dozens of creatures from all around Wholandra gathered to watch the battle. Ines was fast, but the Pharaoh was ferocious. He caught her wing in his teeth and threw her to the ground near the pyramid. A crowd encircled them to see the leader of the city finish off the interloper.

Dylan ran up. "Ines—are you okay?"

"All part of my plan, kitten," Ines panted, bleeding from her lip. "If there's one thing I know how to do, it's get a little publicity."

The crowd around them had grown bigger—the whole city was watching. The Pharaoh's claws slid out. He raised his paw for a death blow.

"Hold on!" Eli shouted. "Dylan—say something! Anything!"

What could he say? If only he had his powers—what could he do without them? He felt words bouncing around his brain like basketballs. *Focus. Focus. Focus.*

Dylan put himself between Ines and the Pharaoh's paw. "Everyone is watching!"

Eli took Dylan's lead. "Pharaoh, if you hurt her, or take us to the Baron, everyone will know you didn't send us home."

"Every Xamaican will know something's screwy with the wishes," Dylan whispered. "They'll know your magic is gone. All your wishcoins won't be worth anything."

The Pharaoh retracted his claws. "What do you propose?" he asked.

"We can get Nanni's book for you. We'll use it to find my sister and the Root of Xamaica. You can use it to replenish your obeah."

The Pharaoh nodded slowly and his guards lowered their spears. "You'll have to go to Robeen Bay."

"Where's that?" Eli asked.

"The Baron took Nanni's book from her," explained the Pharaoh. "He's spent much of his wealth on a temple of magic and learning beneath the waves: the Castle of Wonders."

"Cool!" said Eli. "We're so there."

Ines rose to her feet, bruised and battered. "I wish I had a better feeling about where we're headed."

BOOK THREE

THE QUEEN OF THE DARK INTERVAL

CHAPTER SIXTEEN

One stretch of Hope Road ran along the sea at the foot of a white cliff. The stone formation cast shadows across the way. The smell of sea salt and the sound of the surf were all around, and the air was brilliant with the island light of the afternoon. "Have you ever heard of a *Toljabee*?" Ines asked, as she walked with the boys and the spider.

Eli and Dylan looked at each other and shrugged.

"It's a Korean thing," Ines told them. "Kids do it when they're a year old. Dad was busy, so I didn't have mine until

I was three. My whole family came—even relatives from Seoul. They put all these objects on the table. I had to choose one—and that would foretell my future."

"Oh yeah—I heard this once on NPR," Eli said. "The string means long life. The pen means you'll be a scholar, rice means riches. What did you pick?"

"I don't recall picking anything," Ines replied. "My dad got called away on business. He said we'd finish the ceremony later. We never did. I fell asleep waiting."

Dylan didn't see how this conversation could help them in their search. "You brought this up because . . . ?"

"The shadows reminded me," Ines murmured. "I used to stay up late, waiting for him, hoping I'd see his shadow beneath my bedroom door. It was never there."

Eli frowned. "I totally didn't get that story."

Nestuh slapped him on the back. "But at least it had heart! Stick with me and someday you'll all be master storytellers! It just takes practice. And an ending!"

Dozens of tiny houses were clustered around Robeen Bay like ants around a piece of pie. It had taken the kids about a day's journey on Hope Road to get there. The shacks in Robeen Bay—mostly one-story, ramshackle affairs—were almost too haphazardly arranged to be properly called a town. It looked like instead of being planned and constructed, the community had sprouted up like a clump of weeds.

The kids and Nestuh walked, rolled, crawled, and in Ines's case cat-walked down what now appeared to be Main Street. The town seemed empty, except for trees and shrubbery. "Where is everyone?" Dylan asked.

"Chuh—look again," Nestuh advised.

The trees were moving, and the shrubs too. What at first appeared to be greenery was actually townsfolk. More like greenfolk, actually. They were the size and shape of humans, but their hair was like leaves, their bodies slim stalks, and their feet decidedly rootlike. But they were far from ugly—they had a kind of organic elegance, like a veggie dish at a five-star restaurant. All the plant people were gathering around to give what seemed to be an official town greeting. They moved in an odd swaying walk that resembled the wind moving through a field of sugarcane.

"What are these things?" Eli asked.

"Dem not things," Nestuh answered. "Arrowaks, dem called."

"We saw some of them back at the pyramid," Ines said.

The residents were friendly, almost cloyingly so. They seemed unafraid of Ines in all her Iron Lion–ness (they probably figured, correctly, that she wasn't a vegetarian), and they were downright fond of Nestuh. The villagers put garlands of flowers, fruits, and spices around the necks of the visitors. The wreaths were horribly aromatic, but Nestuh cautioned everyone that it would be rude to refuse the gifts, despite the fact that it was terribly smelly to accept them.

"You guys seem well-stocked," Eli said, holding up a basketful of apples.

"We don't worry about the environment," one stout villager with carrot-orange hair said.

"Have you seen a little human girl lately?" asked Dylan, who was now weighed down with a bucket of naseberries.

"I try not to notice things," one woman carrying a bouquet of passionflowers responded.

"I guess that means they're not worrying that the web is about to fall on their heads in less than two days," Eli said.

"Are you the Root of Xamaica?" Ines asked one of the creatures.

"We don't really put down roots," a man with a bunch of bananas for hair replied. "We're more about fruits."

Ines whispered to Dylan and Eli: "When you get a sec, we need to talk."

One girl, with gray eyes and star apples in her hair, led the travelers through the town and down a path to a nearby field. Or rather, the field was the town. Or perhaps it's better to say the field was the townspeople. There they were, row after row of plant people, quiet, bending with the breeze. As they swayed, they sang a song with silly lyrics, a stupid melody, and a goofy rhythm. The fields of plant people went on for acres. A nation of crops, asking only for sunlight and rain and the occasional dollop of manure.

Soon the girl with the gray eyes brought the children and Nestuh to an empty hut. Compared to the other homes, this one was a palace.

"My name is Zarafina," the star-apple girl said. "This is all for you."

The hut was filled with platters laden with fruits of every sort—mangoes, breadfruit, papaya, oranges, guinep, naseberries, pomegranates, passionfruit, star apples, rose apples, regular apples, pineapples—and Zarafina herself, who, besides having apple cheeks, let it be known that she was the apple of her parents' eyes.

Also on display were a range of amusements: a guitar, a Shatranj set, and more.

Dylan and Eli dove in and started piling plates high with fruit.

Zarafina paid special attention to Dylan. She led him to a stone bench to lie on, and prepared to hand-feed him wedges of passionfruit.

"Getting ready for a fruit break?" Ines asked.

"You bet," Dylan said, moments away from chowing down on a star apple.

"Why don't you ask where it comes from?" Ines cooed.

"We harvest it ourselves," Zarafina explained.

"Sweet," Eli said, who was peeling a piece of breadfruit.

"What she means is they harvest *themselves*," Ines said. "That's not breadfruit. It's *head* fruit."

"You grow this . . ." Dylan began.

"On your heads?" Eli finished.

"Some of it grows on other parts of our bodies as well," Zarafina said. "I picked that breadfruit off someone's b—"

Eli and Dylan put down their plates.

"Exactly," Ines said. She turned to Zarafina. "So where is the Castle of Wonders?"

Zarafina gave her a blank look.

"The cool place beneath the waves where Nanni's book is kept?" Eli prompted.

"Oh—*that* Castle of Wonders. It's on an island just beyond the beach," Zarafina said.

Ines looked skeptical. "Can we just walk in? Is there a gift shop?"

"So many questions! The people of this village don't

concern themselves with such things. The affairs of this world come and go."

"So does the weather," Eli said. "But you can still get wet."

"Can we go to the Castle of Wonders?" Ines asked. "Like now?"

"No, not now," Zarafina answered. "Night is coming. It is time for pleasant dreams. In the morning, when we turn our leaves to the sun, we'll take you there."

"People here don't seem to be worried about much," Ines observed.

"It is the Xamaican way," Zarafina said. "Because we do not dwell on the things that divide us, we have grown ever so close as a nation."

And with that, and a wink at Dylan, the girl left.

CHAPTER SEVENTEEN

"I'm telling you, that tramp is up to something," Ines said.
"She seems pretty cool to me—and nice," Dylan said,
setting up the Shatranj pieces for a game with Eli. It looked
a lot like chess, so they figured they'd give it a try.

"I know nice girls," Ines hissed. "I know bad ones. She
ain't a nice one."

"Meow! I can see why you're half-cat!" Eli cracked,
moving a pawn.

"I'm an Iron Lion. We like to ask questions. Look at you guys! There's danger all around us and you take food from strangers—something that even toddlers don't do—and now you're playing chess!"

"Shatranj, actually," Dylan corrected.

"Hello? Spoiler alert! There's something wrong here," Ines warned. "We need to figure out how to help."

Dylan laughed. "How is any trouble with these plant people our problem?"

Ines pulled out a piece of a crimson feather. "This is what I wanted to talk about. I found it as we were walking into town. Don't you think it's funny that nobody mentioned anything about a huge feathered monster? These plant people are hiding something!"

Dylan and Eli kept playing their game.

"You can't ignore what's happening around us. Your sister is out there somewhere. She could be lost, she could be hurt! You can't lose focus now!" Ines pleaded.

Emma and the Professor always said Dylan was easily distracted. But the fact that Ines had him figured out too made Dylan even more stubborn. He moved a piece that looked like a queen.

"Go ahead. Be irresponsible," said Ines. "You're just like your dad."

Dylan bit his nails. "What do you know about my dad?"

"I have files. Your dad applied for a Mee Corp. job seven years ago."

"Impossible. My parents died in a plane crash nine years ago."

"Is that what they told you?"

Eli was already checking it out on his laptop. "She's not lying—I just hacked the Mee Corp. records. Your dad did work there, but most of his file has been deleted."

Dylan strode up to Ines, his face serious as cancer. "Tell me what else you know."

"I don't want to get into your family business."

"You're already in my business with your stupid files. Now tell me what you know!"

"Your dad was fired from Mee Corp.," Ines said. "His name was Griffith, right? He had been hired to write a fictional field guide for a game the company was producing."

"Wait—my dad wrote the *Xamaicapedia*?"

"He was a paleontologist by training—brilliant but emotionally unstable. That's why he couldn't get a real job at a college. He was supposed to give the guide a touch of reality. Trouble is, he began to act like it was really real. He said writing the guide was triggering memories of stuff he thought he had only imagined. And . . ."

"What? Tell me everything. Why did I not hear from him?"

"He died in an insane asylum."

"You're lying! When?"

"Three years ago. I'm sorry. I thought you knew."

A wave of anger swept through Dylan. All the pieces of his family puzzle, the ones he had been slowly trying, all his life, to turn into a picture, suddenly scattered. He knocked over the Shatranj set and pieces went flying around the room.

Ines bared her Iron Lion teeth. "Do you really want to try me?" she snarled.

141

"If you even think of attacking, you better kill me," Dylan fired back. "I'm pissed, and I'm not friggin' joking around."

Ines's claws slid out of her paws. Dylan picked up a rock. Eli grabbed a banana.

"How are you gonna stop her with that?" Dylan said to Eli.

"Well, if I peel it, maybe she'll slip on it."

There was deadly quiet as the boys and Ines faced off. Then Dylan's stomach growled and broke the silence.

"Never argue on an empty stomach, mon," Nestuh broke in. "That's how two of my aunts ended up eating each other."

Dylan said nothing, but Eli giggled. Although Ines retracted her claws, she still seemed angry. She paced the room on her silent cat's paws. "Stop staring at me!" she yelled at Nestuh.

"Those are markings on my back, mon," Nestuh said. "Dem just look like eyes."

Ines wheeled around and faced the boys. "Listen, I'm sorry about your dad—but you're making a mistake by staying here. And it's your funeral."

She threw the piece of feather at Dylan and stomped away into another chamber in the hut. Dylan picked up the feather and stuffed it in his pocket. If it really was magic, maybe he could use it for something. No way she was getting this back. He was still pissed, and he started biting his fingernails. All this drama hadn't gotten him any closer to finding his sister. He felt tense and his neck was stiff. He was getting too worked up. There was a metallic taste in his mouth—

Suddenly, he was on his back on the dirt floor of the hut.

Eli was standing over him.

"You okay?" Eli asked. "You freaked me out there. I think you had a seizure."

Dylan struggled to his feet. There was blood in his mouth. He had bitten through part of his tongue. "How long was I out?"

"Just a few seconds. But it was bad. Your eyes rolled back and you were flailing around. Dude, it was scary. Should I get Ines in here? She may know—"

"Forget that. And forget her. I just need something to eat. It'll settle me down."

"You heard Ines," Eli cautioned. "We shouldn't eat this stuff."

"I don't care," Dylan said, picking up a star apple. "I'm not listening to her anymore. I'm tired of being antelopes. Let's be lions."

"Lions don't eat fruit."

"You know what I mean."

Dylan took a bite of the star apple and the juice stung his wounded tongue but it was still sweet. He threw Eli a passionfruit, and Eli began to chow down too. As Dylan ate he could feel the scratches on his chest begin to burn. He tried to ignore it and focus on the food—the juice was running down his chin now, and his hands were stained red and purple. It was as if a voice was whispering to him to eat more and eat faster, to give himself over entirely to his appetite.

Outside, the plant people were singing again. Dylan stopped eating.

"Hey, man, are you okay?" Eli asked Dylan.

"You heard what she said. My dad was around all this time—and now he's gone. Why didn't he contact us?"

"He probably stayed away to protect you from whatever demons were driving him. That must have been a nightmare for him."

Silence. "I hate to say it, but Ines is right," Dylan said. "We're all in danger here. I have to stay to find Emma. But I don't get why you're still here."

"How can you say that? You know I always have your back."

"That's not what I'm talking about. Why do you want Nanni's book so bad?"

"Hello? All the wealth of the world?"

"Since when do you care about money? You hate corporations and profits and all that kinda stuff."

"I have my reasons."

"Well?"

"I don't want to talk about it."

"If you're not gonna tell me, who you gonna tell? Remember the first day of middle school? Neither of us had anyone to sit with in the cafeteria. So we sat with each other. We're the two Musketeers, man."

"There were three Musketeers. Maybe even four."

"See? What we have is even more exclusive. So what's up?"

Eli started to cough, and pulled his snuglet closer around him. "You first. Are you gonna tell me what's up with your mystery condition?"

Dylan fell silent.

"Your sickness or whatever? The one your sister mentioned before we left. You gonna tell me about it?"

"Maybe," Dylan said. "But not now."

* * *

A few hours later, Ines came over to the boys' side of the hut. Dylan, still thinking about his father, was wide awake.

"What's going on?" Eli yawned. "It must be three in the morning!"

She opened the door. "You might want to take a look at this."

Eli and Dylan peeked out the door. The townspeople were all lined up outside. Their eyes were white. Their skin was drawn and gray. They weren't plant people now—they seemed more like husks. They were zombies.

"Ines?" Eli asked.

"What?"

"Now would be a good time to tell Dylan *I told you so*."

The townspeople/zombies were singing again, but this time it was angry and menacing like the chanting of pissed-off monks. Zarafina stood in front of the zombies. Fire blazed from her eyes and her hair was also aflame. In one swift move she pulled off all her skin like a lady slipping off a leather glove. Now she was a body of pure fire.

Ines gagged. "That's wrong on so many levels!"

"Now I and I see," Nestuh said. "She's a Soucouyant."

"A Sook-ah-who?" Eli said.

"A Sook-ah-what?" Dylan said.

"She's humanlike by day, and by night she slips out of her skin and becomes a flesh-eating plant," Nestuh explained.

"So she's like a creeper vine," Dylan said. "A human weed."

"Dude, your girlfriend grows on people—literally," Eli said.

"It gets worse, mon," Nestuh added. "If you eat her fruit and fall asleep, she enslaves you. She's turned the town into zombies."

Zarafina now seemed more plant than human. Her mouth and hands looked like Venus flytraps, with yawning openings and spiky fringes. Ivylike tendrils of fire curled around her, writhing and twisting. They snaked out from her body toward the townsfolk, twisting around their limbs and torsos as well. The whole community seemed linked in some viney, creepy, awful way and the Soucouyant was at the center of it. Tongues of flames shot out around her ivy-entwined form.

"Eli—your hand!" Dylan said.

Eli looked at his hand. It was sprouting tiny leaves.

"Did you eat that fruit?" Ines asked.

"S-S-Some," Eli stammered.

"Did you fall asleep?" Dylan asked.

"Absolutely not!" Now fingers on his left hand were twisting and fusing together like rolls of Play-Doh. "Okay, I-I-I may have nodded off."

"Yeah, I think we figured that one out, Pinocchio," Ines said.

Soon the hand had turned green and brown and looked like a leafy vine.

"That thing out there is behind this?" Eli asked.

"Yeah, mon," Nestuh said. "And did I mention Soucouyants shoot fireballs?"

"I've heard of a hot date," Eli said, "but this is just stupid."

Dylan closed the door. "Less talking, more running."

"Where?" Ines asked. "There's only one exit."

"How about an air vent?" Dylan said. "That's what people do in action movies."

Eli shook his head. "What part of *we're in a hut* did you not understand?"

Ines pulled a thick black glove out of her I-Got-Your-Back Pack. "There's this!"

"What's that?" Dylan said.

With his one good hand, Eli was already looking it up on his laptop.

Xamaicapedia:
The Gamer's Guide to Saving the World
A publication of Fiercely Independent Booksellers Inc.
(A wholly owned subsidiary of Mee Corp. Enterprises.)

The Fist of Back-o-Wall: This magic glove can break through any substance. Ideal for breaking though walls, fences, fortifications, and roadblocks. Also suitable for breaking promises, breaking the news, breaking the ice, breaking color barriers, shattering glass ceilings, smashing world records, and coffee breaks. Warning: if used for break dancing, breaking hearts, or breaking wind, please consult a physician and/or lawyer, and maybe crack a window.

Eli grabbed the glove from Ines and slipped it on. His right hand pulsed with energy.

"How did my dad know about this stuff?" Dylan asked.

"Must have had friends in magical places," Eli said.

"Why's there only one glove?" Ines asked.

"Worked for Michael Jackson." Eli punched the wall—and howled in pain. The wall was undamaged.

"Maybe it needs new batteries?" Ines offered.

"You probably need to activate it," Dylan reasoned. "But how?"

"Ohhh! Visualize!" Ines said. "Think of things with holes!"

"Like all the zeros in your bank account?" Eli cracked.

"Or the hole in your head?" Ines shot back.

"Focus!" Dylan snapped. "What about a motorcycle tire? Or a basketball hoop?"

Eli punched the wall again. This time it shuddered, but didn't give way.

"We have to think bigger," Eli said. "What else has a hole?"

"A tornado!"

"The ozone layer!"

"A black hole!"

At that, Eli took another swing—and knocked a hole the size of a car through the back of the hut. Everyone sprinted, scampered, soared, or rolled out. Behind them the hut exploded in flames.

CHAPTER EIGHTEEN

They were lost. As it turned out, the shacks around Robeen Bay weren't randomly placed. The entire village was set on a massive system of gears and pulleys. The streets were an ever-shifting maze. Just when you thought you were on the way out, there would be a horrible grinding of gears, a terrible groaning of ropes, a frightful slamming of gates, and the maze would change again.

Dylan ripped off another strip of fingernail with his teeth. "There better not be a Minotaur at the end of this."

"No, mon, I've met the Minotaur—he's a good guy," Nestuh said. "He gets a bad rap. Besides, he lives on the South Coast."

Ines tried to fly above the maze to get a better look at possible exits. But each time she took wing, the Soucouyant would toss a fireball. Ines's wings were metal, but they couldn't take much more battering. The kids couldn't go up and they couldn't go back.

The maze moved again and the kids were facing a stone wall. Eli punched another hole through it, but even with the Fist of Back-o-Wall the kids couldn't break down walls fast enough.

"Those things are getting closer," Ines said. "I'm sorry guys—about everything. And Dylan—I really apologize for what I said before about your dad. Before he went to the asylum, he worked at Mort World—you know, that theme park run by my dad's biggest competitor—so he dropped off our radar. I didn't realize you didn't know what happened. I didn't mean to hurt you."

"Save it," Dylan said. "Let's focus on finding a way out of here."

"What about the crimson feather?" Eli asked. "We could fly out."

"The last feather we had went up like a match," Ines said. "Maybe you didn't notice, but that thing shoots fireballs."

"Fire—that's it!" Eli declared. "I have a plan!"

"What do you mean?" Ines asked.

"Firewalls!" Eli said. "The game and this world are connected. If I can break through the firewalls, I can hack what's happening to us."

"But you've never been able to hack into Xamaica," Dylan said.

"I've planted a few viruses, but yeah, the firewalls are

pretty much impossible to break through. Anyway, this time I'll have help."

"The Fist of Back-o-Wall can punch through anything . . ." Dylan began.

"Why not firewalls?" Ines exclaimed, finishing the thought. "That's beyond genius!"

Eli pulled out his computer from beneath his wheelchair and starting writing code. Even programming with his gloved hand, things didn't take long. He was able to take control of the moving walls of the maze. With a rumble, a wall in front of them turned and revealed a passageway. "I got this," Eli said. He rolled ahead.

Jabbing away at his keypad, Eli moved walls and opened up paths. He would press a key and a barrier would pop up between the kids and the zombie plants. He'd type in a command and an alleyway would suddenly appear. They could hear the frustrated shrieks of the Soucouyant fading in the distance until they were completely gone.

"His file said he was good, but I didn't know he was *this* good," Ines said. "We need to hire him for Mee Corp.'s IT team!"

At last the kids came to the beach. The moon was out. In fact, both of Xamaica's moons were out, including the ringed one. Huge waves beat against the shore.

The townspeople/zombies were there waiting—and so was the Soucouyant. The kids hadn't escaped—they had been herded to this spot. Plus, scattered across the beach were a number of large crimson feathers. The flying thing, whatever it was, was closer than ever.

"Bummer," Eli said.

His computer shorted out. He shoved it back under his chair and beat down the flames on his lap. Then the Fist of Back-o-Wall caught fire, so Eli peeled it off with the arm of his wheelchair and threw it away. The glove writhed on the ground before turning to ashes.

"I'm sorry, guys. It's like they knew what I was gonna do before I did it." Eli slumped over in his wheelchair, struggling to breathe; his asthma was acting up. They were all trapped. If only Dylan's powers were working—he needed that cheat code more than ever. He had to get some sort of outside help.

"Where's the island?" Ines asked, looking out across the water. "Where's the Castle of Wonders?"

"There will be no wonders for you," the Soucouyant hissed in a voice that was amazingly chilly for a creature made of fire, "and no escape." She held up a book in her left hand. The cover glittered gold in the firelight.

"Nanni's book!" Eli exclaimed.

"This is what you came for, isn't it?" the Soucouyant said, sparks spitting from her mouth. "This is the answer to all your problems. A book worth more than everything in the Great Library of Alexandria! The wealth of the world is inside it."

"It's a tricky-trick!" Nestuh said. "That's what dem firewomen do. Dem take your greatest desires and dem tempt you!"

"Liar! The spider wants the book himself!" the Soucouyant said. "Wealth—that's what you want, isn't it? Health—that's what you need, isn't it? This book is your only hope!"

"Do what you want!" Eli shouted. "I don't need your book!"

"Are you sure about that?" the Soucouyant said slyly, then opened the book. A pillar of fire burst from the pages into the sky. Flames raced across the clouds. Images appeared.

"Don't looky-look!" Nestuh said. "It's a Soucouyant trick."

Dylan stared at the fiery scenes in the sky. He saw Eli's mother and father arguing. Papá's start-ups were always failing and she just couldn't live like that anymore. They were in a lawyer's office signing divorce papers. The scene shifted. Eli's family was moving out of their apartment. His father was going in one car, his mother and little sister Madeleine were in a taxi to the train station. The scene jumped ahead again. There was a train derailment. There were bodies everywhere. Dylan could see Eli's dad arriving at the scene. Mamá and Madeleine: they didn't make it. He sped off in his car. If they hadn't split this wouldn't have happened. He ran a red light. He never saw the snowplow.

The images vanished in a burst of flame and the sky was dark again. Gray smoke billowed out of the smoldering book.

"How do you know so much about my family?" Eli asked.

The Soucouyant cackled. "The Inklings are not the only ones who can bridge the worlds! What you see is what will be unless you stop it. Search your heart—you know this to be true! You need this treasure. You need this book. Or your family dies."

The monster threw the book over the kids' heads and into the sea.

"Nooooooo!" Eli screamed. He lurched from his chair into the water, flailing at the sinking book with his viney arm and one good hand.

"Yes!" the Soucouyant shrieked. "Give in to your greed!"

"No way—I have a pl—"

Eli never finished. The Soucouyant flung a fireball at him and it exploded just as a huge wave hit.

"Eli!" Ines cried.

He had disappeared—incinerated, or taken by the tide. All that was left, lying on the sand, was a sopping-wet snuglet.

CHAPTER NINETEEN

The children moved toward the waves to look for Eli—
but the Soucouyant lobbed a fireball that kept them
away from the water's edge.

"Search in vain!" the Soucouyant mocked. "Your friend
is drowned, or taken by Ma Sinéad, the pirate queen!"

"Why are you attacking us? What did you do to Eli?"
Dylan said. "We've done nothing to you!"

"I am in the service of Baron Zonip," the Soucouyant
sneered.

"We're not your enemies!" Dylan pleaded. "We're not with Queen Nanni! She's tricking you! She probably killed my parents *and* kidnapped my sister! It's all a setup! We didn't set fire to the nest trees!"

The Soucouyant laughed, and her mirth sounded like paper crackling in a fire. "The Baron knows you didn't destroy the nest trees."

"What? How?"

"Because he did it himself."

Dylan was silent.

The Soucouyant laughed her burning laugh again. "The Baron needed an excuse to unravel the Great Web of the World. Such a thing cannot be broken by any singular spell—the collective will of Xamaica maintained it."

"So when the people believed it should come down ..."

"Only then could the Baron bring it down."

"Righteous retribution was the perfect cover," Dylan said.

"And now let the heavens fall," the Soucouyant hissed.

A great tearing rolled across the sky, like gods gone bowling.

"Another corner of the Great Web has fallen!" Nestuh cried.

A ghastly cheer rose up from the zombies that was quite the opposite of cheerful.

"Now only two threads remain," the Soucouyant said. "And not for long. All of Xamaica will hear how a Babylonian boy and his untrustworthy companions staged a jailbreak at Robeen Bay—and perished in the attempt. They will rally around the Baron for protection, and give him the support he requires to tear down the rest of the Great Web. There will be no principles left. The Baron will be free to enlist soldiers, enslave citizens, and slay any who oppose him. And then the way will be clear for his ultimate plan."

"What about Nanni? The Confederacy of Shadows? I thought this was about stopping her!"

"Ha! The Baron defeated Nanni when you arrived here," the creature laughed. "And now you will be vanquished as well."

"The Pharaoh betrayed us," Ines sobbed. "I guess there were too many witnesses for him to execute us back in Wholandra. I can't believe Eli is gone!"

A chant went up from the zombies: "Fight! Fight Fight!" The Soucouyant's hands filled with flame.

"Her next fireball is going to finish us," Ines cried.

"You were right," Dylan said. "I shouldn't have tasted the fruit. I shouldn't have lost focus!"

"Now," the Soucouyant screeched, "prepare to go not to a Castle of Wonders, but to a House of Horrors!"

The Soucouyant reared back, ready to throw her fireball. But suddenly the waters rose—and rose. In a few moments, the night was filled with a wall of wet—and all that water was immediately released. The huge wave came down on the beach as if the earth and sea had changed places. The zombies were smashed against the rock. The Soucouyant screamed and was extinguished.

A weird humming filled the air.

"That's what my dad used to . . ." Ines started to say. Then she and Dylan saw it—there, in the middle of the waves, a shadow fell across the water. It slowly approached them, making neither a splash nor a ripple.

"Dad?" Ines said.

My little warrior, the shadow said. *Trust me if you want to live.*

CHAPTER TWENTY

The shadow sunk beneath the waves.

"Was that your dad's shadow?" Dylan asked. "Should we follow?"

Ines had stopped at the water's edge—she was crying. Dylan put an arm around her. "I know how you feel. We might have lost Eli, we haven't found Emma. Why bother with anything?"

"I just want to go home. But I don't even have one anymore."

"What do you mean?"

She didn't answer and peered at her reflection in the rippling surface.

"Mee Corp. is bankrupt," she murmured. "We're, like, beyond broke. There'll be a big press conference when we get back. It'll all be gone soon. I'm sure somewhere in Mort World, Mort Clemens is laughing."

"Bankrupt? What about flying hairdressers in from Dubai and all that stuff?"

Ines sighed. "Everything isn't everything. Money seems so pointless next to everything we've lost here. I just worry about my Global Friends—the kids I support with my charity."

"Is this connected to that globe you didn't want Emma to touch at the mansion?"

"That's how I keep in touch with them, yeah. Who's going to take care of them if Mee Corp. is broke?" Ines buried her face in her paws.

Dylan picked up the snuglet, which wept seawater. It was hot, like the damp towels they give you at Japanese restaurants. The fireball hadn't even left any ashes. How could his best friend in the world—in any world—just vanish like that? Dylan felt sick and impossibly sad, like his heart was being gripped by a fist. "Maybe we should follow your dad's shadow. I don't see the point of staying here."

"My dad never told me anything. He never took me anywhere. He let Mee Corp. go bust. And now he says to trust him. I don't know what to think."

"So you think it's really him? Or is it a trap?"

Nestuh skittered up to Ines and Dylan. "You must make a decision or the shadow will be too far away for us to follow it."

Ines kept looking out over the waves where crimson

feathers floated on the surface. Then she shuddered and dove in.

Dylan, Ines, and Nestuh followed the shadow beneath the waves. Several Watas swam in the sea around them. They found that if they stayed close to the Watas they could all breathe underwater. They could even talk.

"I wonder why they're helping us," Ines said.

"We were the only ones who were ever nice to the Wata Mamas, I guess," Dylan shrugged.

The dark form remained just ahead. Even as they swam, its strange voice carried back to them.

The book was an illusion, said the voice. *Wealth is an illusion. Lao-tzu said the wise man accepts his nemesis as the shadow that he himself casts.*

"Where are you taking us?" Dylan asked. "Do you know where my sister Emma is?"

"Stop—we have to talk!" Ines commanded.

I've waited for this moment. A shadow can only stay if it anchors itself to a single thought. One word was in my mind: daughter.

They had moved far out to sea, and had gone deep down. But they could sense something happening on the surface.

A reddish glow was moving along the face of the water. It was a massive ball of crimson light, many times bigger than any sea dragon or Iron Lion or indeed any creature the children had seen in Xamaica. Even from the bowels of the sea, the children could feel the power of the beast's movements, feel the beat of its vast wings—and hear the reverberations of its roar.

By leading them beneath the water, the shadow had saved them from encountering whatever creature was behind that horrid howl.

"I've heard that roar before," Dylan said. "That's the thing that attacked the *Black Starr*."

Ines put a paw against his cheek. "There's something else. Back at Mee Corp., your dad told human resources a flying dinosaur had crashed his plane and its venom was slowly killing him. Everyone thought he was crazy. That's why he was fired. But from the looks of that thing, he was on to something."

Two sharp pains—a cold blue hurt, like frostbite—shot across Dylan's torso. He clutched at his scratches. His dad wasn't crazy. Whatever this thing was, he would kill it and avenge the parents he couldn't even remember. He began to rise to the surface.

Nestuh put a leg on his shoulder and held Dylan back.

"Let me go!" Dylan protested. "I have to fight it. I want to kill it!"

"Nuh, mon, not now," Nestuh advised. "We have chosen to follow the shadow. He who fight and swim away, lives to fight another day. Unless, of course, him drown."

So they kept going. They couldn't get a clear view of the thing through the shimmering surface of the water. But it seemed to be bearing a load.

The things it carried fell without a splash.

The beast was dropping shadows.

Some strange obeah was at work. Without weight, the shadows sank through the water. Without a sound, they drifted down into the far fathoms. Without resistance, chains extended and bound them.

Follow me, my little warrior, the shadow of Ines's father said.

The children and the spider dove deeper into the waters.

"Talk to me!" Ines urged. "What was that thing?"

The shadow stealer. The crimson beast. The feathered thing from a billion yesterdays.

"Where are we going?" Ines asked.

I must tell you everything—from the beginning, because we are near the end.

"Stop swimming for a second," Ines said.

But the shadow kept moving and speaking and hurriedly heading toward its unknown destination.

When I started Mee Corp., your mother and I sold gadgets out of a small shop in Seoul. She would write songs in her spare time, and I would tinker on my inventions. But it wasn't enough for me. I began borrowing heavily to help grow the business. I swore I would give anything to succeed. It was then that a package arrived. Inside was a single black tablet. There was a note with it: Play me.

"Xamaica," Dylan said.

The tablet contained just ten lines of computer code. But I quickly realized the programming was so powerful, so unlike anything that had been seen before, I could use it to form the foundation for the greatest game the world had ever seen. My wife begged me to have nothing to do with it. It was around this time that she gave birth to you. I hurried from work to the hospital—but she died in my arms. I was still in my lab coat and goggles—and, except to clean them, I haven't taken them off since. I was a single father, and I had to provide for my baby. I used the code on the tablet and began selling the game.

"I'm so sorry about your mom," Dylan said to Ines.

"But this also means my dad didn't rip off Eli's dad. The Baron did."

Eli will probably never know, Dylan thought grimly. He was gone, like Emma. He was losing everyone.

The first shipment sold out. I opened two new shops to keep up with demand. Soon, business was booming and we moved to America.

"Didn't you wonder where the game came from?" asked Ines.

Every few months, a Xamaica upgrade would appear in the mail. I grew wary, and began to throw the packages in my fireplace. One day, a stranger arrived at my door with a hooded cloak and glowing red eyes.

"Higues," Dylan said. "Servants of the Baron."

He had in his hand the package, miraculously unburned, I had destroyed the night before. I knew then I had made a terrible mistake getting involved in Xamaica. I was convinced that the stranger was the front man for a larger evil. I demanded to know the game's ultimate purpose. He said three words: We shall see. *Then he disappeared.*

"What? That's it?" Dylan said.

"No—I saw the stranger in his office the night my dad disappeared," Ines said.

Shadows have lost their bodies. We must anchor ourselves in thought.

Ines plowed ahead. "My whole life, you were always just out of reach—I'm not going to let you leave now!" she cried.

The shadow stopped, turned, and she embraced it. Or tried to.

Her arms passed right through it.

The game was no game, said the shadow. *The Baron tricked me into making his portal. He wanted to send agents to Earth— for what end I do not know. When I tried to stop the madness, he attacked. The Baron has mastered a terrible obeah. With it, he can separate his enemies from their shadows. Our shadows embody our dreams. Torn in two, our bodies wither away. He stole my shadow, and my body fell into a dreamless daze.*

"So Nanni isn't behind the Confederacy of Shadows," Dylan said. "It was the Baron all along."

"That must have been the flash of light I saw beneath your office door just before you collapsed," Ines said. "The giant crimson feather must have been from the beast. The Baron is behind the beast, not Queen Nanni. But why is he stealing shadows? What's he doing with them?"

I left clues for you to find me. But my body is beyond all assistance. One word kept me: daughter.

"Why didn't you tell me anything before? About Xamaica?"

I was trying to protect you. You are my greatest invention! That is why I created your show. So you could have adventures and never be harmed.

"You just didn't want to deal with me! You didn't want to deal with questions about the company, which was a total fraud!"

I thought that someday Mee Corp. could make the game without the Baron. I didn't know we were part of a devilish scheme. I never tried to cheat anyone—you have to believe me!

"Why should I believe you? Everything you've said is a lie!"

Because I want to make it right. She can do that. She knew others would come for me. She released me when she could not save herself.

"Who is *she*?"

You must find her. You must find the Root. I'm so sorry.

"Dad—you're beginning to fade. Where are you going?"

Do you believe in me? the shadow asked.

Ines tried to grab hold of him.

My little warrior.

"Why do you keep calling me that?"

It's what you picked at your Toljabee. *You fell asleep waiting for me, and when I came home, you had it clutched in your hand. You never knew, but you made your choice as you dreamt. An arrow. It meant you were a warrior. My little warrior.*

"So you came back! You did come back!"

But then he was gone. Ines was left holding only water.

Ines's mouth opened into a soundless roar of rage and sadness.

As the Watas swam around them, Dylan and the spider hugged Ines and held her tight beneath the waves.

Dylan found his own thoughts drifting back to his sister. He had felt so angry at her, and now he felt ashamed and heavyhearted. Emma was gone, and Eli too. He had never felt grief like this, and it weighed down on his chest like the fathoms of water above him.

Ines swam away.

"Where are you going?" Dylan asked.

"My dad said the book we saw was an illusion," Ines said. "That means the real book is still out there—maybe in the Castle of Wonders. And maybe the Root—whatever it is—is there too. My dad is gone—but it doesn't have to be forever. We just need the right magic. Maybe if we can find the book and the Root . . ."

Dylan put a finger to her lips.

Some creature was swimming toward them. And it was humongous.

CHAPTER TWENTY-ONE

In the lower depths swam a huge glowing thing. The water around it bubbled like it was boiling. The beast had horns, a snout, and hoofs. Its eyes were flaming.

Dylan and Ines began to swim frantically for the surface. Whatever was waiting for them up there couldn't be worse than what was lurking down deep.

"Dude!"

Dylan stopped swimming and looked back.

"What is it?" Ines asked.

"It's Eli!" Dylan answered.

Eli had become a Rolling Calf.

"Sweet!" Dylan gave his friend a fist bump. Or, rather, a fist-to-hoof bump.

Nestuh gave Eli a warm embrace.

"You didn't really think I was gone, did you?" Eli laughed. "I still need storytelling lessons!"

If Ines's face hadn't already been submerged in seawater, it would have been wet and salty with tears. "I'm so glad you're alive!"

"Of course I'm alive," said Eli, who had obviously been cured of the Soucouyant's vine spell. "I'm my true Xamaican self."

Eli told Dylan and Ines his story. His snuglet had saved him. The new company that made them had a better safety record than Mee Corp.—now the snuglets were flame retardant. Plus, at the last second, Eli had had the bright idea to soak the snuglet in seawater to protect himself from the fireball. He hadn't gotten burned too badly, but he was knocked into the waves. He had followed the book down through the deep water. He realized it was crazy doing what he was doing. He couldn't walk much less swim. But Nanni's book was just there at the tips of his fingers. He thought of his family—the images the Soucouyant had shown: the divorce, the derailment—and it was all because of money. He had to get that book. If he could only move a little faster, reach out a little farther. The book was glowing. He could see it pulsing just in front of him, all golden-green in the undersea light.

Deeper and deeper they both fell—the book and the boy. He didn't know if he was alive or dead. He was drowning as he sunk further beneath the waves. He let himself sink.

That's when he thought of his mama and papa. They never gave up. Not when Papá's businesses fizzled and money was tight and things were hopeless.

He realized he had to go back. His friends were still in danger, so the book would have to wait. He could sense watery creatures all around him. They buoyed him, and brought him to the surface. His lungs filled with air and the creatures swam away. Some sort of magic was in him. He felt like a tadpole becoming a frog, or a caterpillar becoming a butterfly, multiplied by the speed of light. His feet became hoofs, horns sprouted from his head, and a mane grew out of his scalp. Steam poured out of his nose and mouth. He was a Rolling Calf. Watas all around him, he dove back down deep looking for his friends.

"So where do we go now?" Dylan asked.

There was no time to celebrate Eli's return. Ines was already swimming deeper.

Now they saw where the shadows went.

Beneath the blue and green of the sea, past the yellow and green of the coral reefs, atop the tan and gray surface of the sea floor, there was a strange shifting spot.

If Dylan hadn't been looking for it, he might have swum right past it. But now that he'd beheld it, he would never forget it. "The Baron didn't spend his riches on a Castle of Wonders," Dylan observed, looking around. "He used it to build a prison of shadows."

The prison's walls were tall and black and ever-shifting. The gate was wide, and topped with jagged spikes. Inside were endless rows of cells, each one enclosed by black bars which shimmered in the vagrant undersea light. It might have been elegant, perhaps even beautiful, had it not been so ominous.

Behind every barred gate there was another shadow. These shadows were alive: there were long shadows and short ones, squat shadows and skinny shadows, shadows with long talons and ones with blunt hooves.

Some shadows seemed in agony, and beat their heads against shadow walls. Others seemed in despair, and bent their heads back to howl shadowy screams.

Many prisoners were fastened to dungeon walls with ebon chains. A few were held in dark stockades. Still others were pinned down in writhing masses by weighted nets.

"I wish we could help these prisoners somehow," Ines said.

"They're just shadows," Dylan replied. "We can't even touch them."

"The book is here somewhere," Eli said. "I can feel the magic."

"After all we've been through, you're still after that book?" Ines complained.

Then, on some lower frequency, something entered their thoughts.

(Krik krak)

Dylan, Eli, and Ines exchanged glances. Something was broadcasting into their minds.

It was a faint voice, but a sure one—it had a steady,

meditative quality. It was like a whisper; not in the ear, but in the heart. Someone, something, was relaying important information to maintain a center in the midst of chaos, punishment, and imprisonment.

(Krik krak)

"A shadow has to anchor itself in one thought," Ines said.

"So whoever this is has anchored themselves in that phrase," Dylan said. "My sister!"

Rushing away, they tried to follow the voice. It seemed to be calling them in a certain direction. Dylan, Nestuh, and Eli, with the Wata Mamas all around them, passed through the shadow prison. Ines swam out in front. Every so often a shadow would swim up to them as if searching for its lost body and then drift away in wordless disappointment.

(Krik krak)

The prison was getting darker. Perhaps this was the high-security wing. The walls were as impenetrable as sleepless nights.

"We have to keep going!" Dylan urged.

"We're close to something important," Ines agreed.

At last, Ines stopped swimming. Whether she had reached her breaking point or their destination they did not know. All around was blackness.

(Krik krak)

"Emma? Emma?" Dylan called.

There was something blacker than the surrounding darkness. There, up ahead. A tall shadow. It loomed above them.

Dylan pointed to Nestuh.

CHAPTER TWENTY-ONE

The markings on the spider's back were suddenly coming alive.

"Someone meant for us to come here," Dylan said.

The spider's markings, which had looked like eyes, now became a face and a body, wrapped in a dark cloak.

(Krik krak)

Now the body and the shadow joined together.

The eyes opened.

For a moment Dylan thought he was staring into Emma's eyes. And then not.

Her appearance was balanced between youth and old age. She had full lips, high round cheeks, and an angled nose with deep creases around her nostrils. Her skin was the color of the red-brown dirt of Xamaica. Her gaze had the hard, cold glint of starlight. Her expression was still and sour, like a bowl of lemons. She could only be Queen Nanni.

Dylan, Ines, and Eli recoiled in horror. Queen Nanni was almost certainly a villain, perhaps a murderer, and definitely alive. They should have seen this coming—if this prison held Nanni's book, why shouldn't it also hold Nanni herself? Now, unwittingly, they had released Xamaica's greatest enemy. Now they were deep underwater, lost, alone, and completely defenseless. They had walked—or more accurately, swum—right into her trap.

Dylan tried to launch himself at her, to attack, but some enchantment around her held him and the others in place. They were caught as easily as a fly on a frog's tongue. The children could not hear what the sorceress uttered next, but they sensed her words in their hearts.

(Krik krak) she said. (Nanni's back)

CHAPTER TWENTY-TWO

(A re you wizards?)
Nanni's words rang clear and cold in the children's heads, like ice cubes clinking and clattering in an empty glass. Her crimson hair wrap, piled high on her head, made her seem even more towering, imposing, and witchy.

"No, Your Majesty, them just kiddy-kids," said Nestuh, who had recovered himself a bit and now stood between Nanni and her visitors from Babylon.

"I'm Ines Mee. So far this year, my name is the 227th most searched-for term on the web."

"Is it just me or are your numbers falling?" Eli muttered.

(By the Inklings! You are neither wizards nor warriors! Ahh—the shame of it) Her lips didn't move, but everyone heard what she said, an instant message to the brain.

"I keep hearing that name—who are the Inklings?" Eli asked.

(They are the world-builders, the dream-makers, the ones that bridge the stars with thought. Had they loosed me, I might have been content. But I have been freed by mere mortals. Are you, at the very least, of royal blood?)

"I hacked into Buckingham Palace once," Eli said. "Fun fact about the Queen of England: Googles herself at least ten times a day."

(Oh—I see. You are jesters and fools, sent to amuse me!)

"We come for a purpose," Ines said. "I seek the Root of Xamaica."

(Then you have found her)

"I don't understand. You're the Root?"

"Fruit are some, branch is others . . ." Nestuh began.

(. . . the Root am I) Nanni finished.

"Why shouldn't we attack you?" Dylan asked. "How do we know you're not responsible for a whole variety of crimes?"

(Because if I wanted to kill you, I would have done so already)

"She has a point there," Eli admitted. "A frightening point, but a point."

(Hold your tongues. You are babes, too young even for the Crimson Vision. The time has come for us to take our leave)

"Where are we going?" Dylan asked.

"What about your book?" Eli said. "What about Nanni's book?"

(Shut up! Speak when spoken to, jester. Now follow!)

With a sweep of her black robe, Queen Nanni turned away.

"Did we not just free her from a magical prison?" Eli said to Dylan and Ines. "A *please* or *thank you* would be nice!"

"I know, right? I can't believe I came all this way and the Root isn't a thing, it's a person," Ines said. "And a really horrible person to boot. She's like the Wicked Witch of the West Indies. How is that gonna help my dad?"

"I don't think your father was looking for help for himself," Eli said. "I think he thought she could somehow help Xamaica."

"Don't talk about my dad in the past tense," Ines said sharply. "Eli's back, right? There's hope for my dad and your sister. We just need the right magic."

Dylan could feel more obeah in the air. "Something's happening."

Nanni waved her right hand and the sea opened up. She raised her left hand and her sleeve slipped down her long, lean arm; a great filmy sphere formed, glistening like a soap bubble in a bath, but as large as a bus. Nanni dropped her arms and bent over in exhaustion. For a second, her years seemed to catch up to her, and she appeared to be unimaginably old. Then her youthful appearance reblossomed, if that's even a word, and she slowly stood upright. With a grand gesture, Nanni motioned for the children to enter the bubble, which hovered slightly above the exposed seabed.

"Dude—do we have to go?" Eli asked.

"It's either that or drown," Dylan answered.

"I'm not certain which is worse," Ines said. "I have to

admit, though, she looks beyond awesome for her age. I guess two thousand is the new twenty."

The children squeezed into the bubble, which closed behind them as each one got in. The bubble then rose above the seabed, above the water, and, quickly and silently, floated across the waves, through the air, and beyond the clouds.

Below and behind them, the shadow prison was still very much intact. Nanni had great power, but even her abilities had their limits. Such a deep spell was woven through the walls of the jailhouse that even she couldn't simply topple it. Instead, she and the others fled. The shadow inmates looked up from the depths mournfully as the children flew away.

"What about the prisoners?" Ines asked. "Aren't they your army? Why are you leaving them behind?"

(Address me as *Your Majesty*!)

"You've got to be kidding!" Ines said. "You're becoming a royal pain in my . . ."

Queen Nanni's eyes glittered, chilly as starlight.

"Nope, you're so not kidding," Ines said. "Okay, I'll play this game. What about all the people that went to prison because of you that you left behind while you made your getaway—Your Majesty."

Nanni ignored Ines's sarcastic tone. (Jester, there are things you couldn't possibly understand. To make them whole and lift them from this place will take deep concentration. I will need my book)

"So your book isn't lost!" Eli said.

(Nothing is lost that cannot be found, jester)

Dylan couldn't trust this witch, but he had to ask: "My sister is missing. Have you seen a human girl?"

(No) Nanni said. (But if she is gone, then it is likely the Baron has her. He seeks to intercept visitors from your world. There are so many missing in these times. She is but one of many)

The words hit Dylan like a fist. His sister—a prisoner. They had spent all this time searching for her—and she was probably being held in the first kingdom they visited. He tried to push all his questions about his dad and the *Xamaicapedia* out of his mind to focus on the task at hand. A gloom came down on his brain like a curtain at the end of a play. He couldn't bear to think of Emma hurt, or imprisoned. Many of the times he had yelled at her—or made fun of her—flashed through his mind. The time they had that mix-up at that stupid pirate party; the time when she correctly answered a question in math class that he had just gotten wrong; the time when—the time when . . . there were so many and they all seemed to mean so much then, but now they just seemed mean.

"It'll be okay, man," Eli said to Dylan, sensing how upset he was. "We'll find her."

The bubble kept floating along. The children peered through the glistening curved surface at the world below. This was the other side of Xamaica. This was across the tracks, how the other half lived, the lower frequencies. The blue waters and green hills were gone. The land was gray and dead. The trees were leafless or fallen or simply stumps. The rivers had dried up and the riverbeds were muddy and the riverbanks were littered with the skeletons of creatures that had perished from thirst. Fields that once boasted rows of sugarcane were now acres of dirt and weeds. The air smelled like the parts of the fish you don't eat, and garbage that you forgot to take out, and armpits you had neglected to deodorize.

"What happened here?" Ines asked.

(When Xamaicans have a funeral, we invite neighbors to pay respect by gathering on the lawn—we call it the Dead Yard. The land here was lush. Now it is all the Dead Yard)

"Why are you draining all the magic?" Dylan asked.

(You have been told a lie. The Baron has done this, not me)

The gray landscape was dotted with vast pits which vomited up sulfurous white scum. The children saw Soucouyants entwined with hundreds of other creatures who had been turned into zombies. The Soucouyants' vines slithered around necks and limbs, and their servant undead were all set to working on menial tasks—breaking rocks, digging pits, hacking at stumps, loading bird dung into buckets. The horrid screeches of the Soucouyants rang across the Dead Yard.

The children could hear another sound too. It was the faint beat of a drum, growing louder, in the far distance. The rhythm was like low thunder, and it seemed to fill the sky and shake the earth.

(Silence, jesters, and listen!) Nanni commanded. (It is the Great Drum of Anancy)

"Then the legends are true!" Nestuh said. "The Great Drum was stolen from my people after the making of the Great Music!"

In the dark, Dylan looked out at the faint flames across the surrounding countryside. There seemed to be as many fires as there were stars in the sky.

"He's using the drum to call the creatures of Xamaica," Dylan said.

(The Baron has raised an army against us)

"Um . . . us?" Eli asked. "The way I see it, there's Team Nanni, and Team Everyone Not Named Nanni."

(Fear not, jester. We're going to a hidden city)

CHAPTER TWENTY-THREE

They headed out over where the land was healthy again, and the Dead Yard receded. It was midday and the sun was bright, the sky was blue, and the clouds were fat and lazy. Dylan and his companions were far from the sea-sprayed coastal terrain of Robeen Bay. Around them were the mist-shrouded peaks of the Blue Mountains.

The bubble popped a few feet above the ground and Dylan and his friends tumbled out. Nanni landed nimbly on her feet, like a gymnast finishing a routine.

(This was the home of the Maruunz—the greatest warriors this world has seen. When they come of age, they get the Crimson Vision, and none may withstand them. They served me and would not serve the Baron—so he destroyed them all. Now they are all shadows—imprisoned in the place you found me)

Then she did something odd: she stopped and gave Nestuh a hug, which he returned with all eight legs.

(Gratitude for returning me to myself) Nanni said, before turning away.

Now they were in Nanni Town, high in the Blue Mountains in the center of Xamaica, the witch informed them. Released from Nanni's spell, they were free to move about as they liked. They stood in front of a small hut with cedar-plank walls and a palm-frond roof. They walked forward to the lip of a place called Pumpkin Hill. Near the edge, a great mahogany rod had been plunged into the earth; on its tip was perched an abeng, a wind instrument made from a cow's horn. A palm tree was planted near the center of the hill, beside the hut. The branches swayed although there was no wind. The trunk undulated like a hula dancer. The whole tree emanated a soft golden radiance. You know how people have a glow after they've just come back from a great Caribbean vacation, or if they've hit the winning free throws in a big game, or they've just won the tri-county spelling bee? The tree had a glow like that—only with actual light.

"That tree is beyond beautiful," Ines said.

"It planted by Nanni," Nestuh informed her. "It is the Great Palm of Protection. All the others, dem seeds of this. As long as it is rooted in the earth, the town cannot be found by those who wish it ill."

Nanni Town may have been beautiful, but Dylan didn't

care. His sister could be sitting in some cell somewhere. The day was warm, but he felt chilly. The air was clean, but he might as well have been breathing in the reek of a moldy basement. His face felt wrong, like he was wearing a plastic Halloween mask of a smile instead of the howl of joylessness reverberating inside him. Yet even though he felt as numb as a novocained tooth he had to keep looking. Emma was out there somewhere.

Dylan stepped to the edge of Pumpkin Hill. He could see now that he was on the top of a great stone ridge with a commanding view of a town beneath. There were several hundred houses, most constructed with walls of wattle and plaster with wooden doors and thatched roofs. A clear stream ran through town, the Macungo, and, at the fringes of town, it poured over a great precipice into the Stony River, which flowed underneath the drop. Where the rivers converged, the water was thrown up with much violence and froth. It seemed to Dylan that, within the seething water, he could glimpse a massive bubbling cauldron.

"It Nanni that make it so," Nestuh said. "She has higher science. She catch musket ball out of air and fire it back, double speed. In her hut on Pumpkin Hill, Nanni has a book of obeah. The book is made of gold and the pages of fire. She cut her vein with a knife and wrote the words in hot blood. There is great science in this book. It make rivers flow backward, goats fly, and duppies return to their trees."

"So the Soucouyant didn't have the real book!" Eli exclaimed. "I knew it!"

"How long have you been in her service?" Ines asked Nestuh.

"Ever since the Baron began to work against Xamaica and not *for* it," Nestuh replied.

"I thought Nanni was the villain," Eli said.

"The world always shifty-shifty," Nestuh shrugged. "Making sure you're in the right is hard as fighting for it. Truth."

"But she's a jerk!" Ines said. "I can't believe you're on a hugging basis with her!"

Nestuh tapped his own chest. "Her heart is scarred. But it beats true."

"How did you know we would wind up at the shadow prison?" Dylan asked.

"I knew, once you were on Hope Road, that it would happen. All roads lead to Nanni. She is what Xamaica needs now."

"You should have told us what you were up to," Eli spat. "You betrayed us!"

"No, mon, I saved you!"

Fire sprang up all around Eli. Nestuh had to jump back to avoid being singed.

"I should burn you to ashes right here," Eli seethed, his eyes aflame. "You tricked us and hand-delivered us to this witch."

If a spider could look stricken, Nestuh would have. "You've seen the sufferers!" he cried. "We need a revolution—so we had to have Queen Nanni's help!"

"Now you're a revolutionary?" Eli scoffed. "I don't know who or what you are! All I know is I'll never trust you again. Never!"

At that, tears poured out of Nestuh's many eyes.

CHAPTER TWENTY-THREE

Ines laid a paw on his dreadlocked head. "You've hurt his feelings!"

"He's lucky I don't have bug spray," Eli jeered. "You're a traitor, Nestuh, hear me? You're not my friend. And what kind of spider can't even spin a friggin' web?"

That seemed to wound Nestuh most and he hid his face behind four of his legs.

Dylan shook his head. "Harsh."

"Necessary," Eli shot back.

Nestuh wiped away his tears. "It's true—I cannot spin or weave or tie. But some knots need to be untied." With that, he skittered away behind a group of huts.

"I'm a hacker—I hate secrets," Eli said. "So Nestuh kept us in the dark—that's his prerogative. But I'm done being his friend. Just like he says—the most important part of a story is knowing when it's over."

From his place of hiding, Nestuh sobbed louder.

Dylan and his friends kept walking with Nanni. Farther beyond the town, Dylan could see acres of farmland, patches of green on green, and the familiar wave of sugarcane stalks swaying in the wind. The town, the streets, and the fields were empty. Even the shadows were gone. As Dylan looked into the distance, Nanni spoke softly into his ear. Her words were low and soothing. He turned to face her and was surprised to see her standing some paces away, her mouth closed, staring serenely out onto the fields.

(Come with me, all of you)

They moved past the many one-story houses, squat and sturdily built, past the clusters of banana trees; near the center

185

of the town, they strolled underneath the Tree of Life, a tree whose trunk was larger than a big man's encircling arms and whose dome-shaped top sprouted blue flowers at the tips of every branch. They rambled on toward the fields outside of town, strolling through the rows of lentil, potatoes, and corn.

(The Baron has been searching for warriors to add to his armies. He enslaves the ones he can use, and destroys the ones he fears may one day oppose him)

"So Xamaica—the video game, that is—is a way for the Baron to capture kids from our world and force them into his service in this world?" Ines speculated. "That explains why not all the forty-four Game Changers showed up at the tournament! The Baron probably already had them!"

"Mee Corp. is like an interdimensional child-slavery ring," Eli said. "Your shareholders are gonna be pissed."

(From Time Out of Mind, it has been said that Jah will bring champions to Xamaica. I monitor the passages between worlds, and I was prepared for your coming. But the Baron was laying in ambush. He has taken a terrifying form. Fortunately, Ma Sinéad came to my aid and sent her ship, the *Black Starr*, to intercept you. The Baron rose to attack and we fought a great contest. But my efforts had a cost, and my defenses were lowered. He stole my shadow and imprisoned it in Robeen Bay. My corporal form was reduced to dust—or so the Baron thought. He did not know that some of the spiders remained loyal to me)

"I still can't believe Nestuh is a friend of yours!" Eli blurted out.

(I have no need for friendship! But spiders can recognize

a web of lies when they see one. Nestuh volunteered to carry my essence on his back until it was reunited with my shadow and I was reborn. To protect him, his memory of our pact was wiped until his mission was completed. While in my service, Nestuh's own family disowned him. But the spider completed his task, as he promised he would. He was able to get you on Hope Road and guide you to me)

"So why are you trying to help people and fight the Baron?" Dylan asked. "All the legends say you're the villain. Why should we trust you now?"

(I have seen other worlds, and now I follow only The Way)

"Did you carve that inscription? *Give your life—and you will find it?*"

(There is obeah in those words. They were passed down from the Inklings long ago. When you overstand what they mean, you will understand what they say. Trust my actions. I will go back to the shadow prison. I will liberate the Maruunz warriors. Then I will have an army to oppose the Baron)

"Wait a second—you're leaving?" Eli asked.

(Address me as Your Majesty!) hissed Nanni, baring her teeth in a sudden fury.

"Whoa!" Eli said. "Chill—Your Majesty. With a temper like that, you must not have many friends!"

Those words seemed to sting Nanni. (I had companionship—long ago and far away) she murmured, half to herself. (But enough of such talk. I leave tonight, though—by the Inkings!—I shall return. Look for me when the shadows are darkest)

"Where are you going?" Dylan shouted after her. "What if the Baron attacks? What do we do?"

Something like a smile flickered on Nanni's lips. (Resist)

Dylan wanted to ask her about the cheat code. But with everyone watching he didn't want to just blurt everything out. "I thought I had powers in Xamaica. But nothing seems to work. How do I get them back? Can you cast a spell or something?"

(Why are you looking to others to find something in yourself?) With that, she vanished into the night.

"She's gone!" Eli gasped. "We're so screwed."

"Calm down," Ines advised. "This is a hidden city, remember?"

There was a new sound in the surrounding woods. Something was out there—a *lot* of somethings.

"Okay, now we're officially screwed," Dylan said.

CHAPTER TWENTY-FOUR

There were eyes in the woods. And a group of whatsits or whosthats or somethingsomethings. They had heads, arms, legs, bodies—and weapons. Knives, swords, crossbows, throwing stars—basically, every fighting tool you can name and a few you probably can't. The strangers were in the shadows but now they stepped into the light.

They were children, no older-looking than Dylan, Ines, and Eli. They were dressed in uniforms the crimson color of the Xamaican earth. They each had long, flowing dreadlocks, which fell down their shoulders like a lion's mane. And they had the most amazing tattoos—full-color pictures that moved cinematically across their skin, recounting, it appeared, the personal histories of each warrior.

"Talk about human highlight reels," Eli said.

The warrior kids were in two groups. On one side were boys, on the other, girls.

"I am Cudgel," pronounced one of the children, a boy. "We are the Maruunz."

"I am Carving Knife," declared another, a girl. "*We* are the Maruunz."

Of all the Maruunz, Cudgel and Carving Knife had the most living tattoos; their tats showed them hunting animals, chasing intruders—and sometimes fighting each other.

"If you're Maruunz, how come your eyes aren't red?" Dylan asked.

"A Maruunz's eyes only get the Crimson Vision when they come of age," Cudgel said. "But trust me, *we're* Maruunz. Those posers over there are just girls."

Carving Knife threw three of her namesake weapons. They slipped through the air like whispers. Each of the knives—all made of stone—lodged in the ground mere millimeters away from Dylan and his companions.

"Okay," Eli exhaled, "you've got skills."

"Why are you split into groups—boys and girls?" Dylan asked.

Cudgel looked grim. "Because only boys are allowed to train to become warriors."

"Ignore my brother," Carving Knife said. "The first Maruunz were men *and* women."

"A woman hasn't gotten the Crimson Vision for a generation."

"So what? There's no reason not to let us train too."

"We've defeated you in three straight skirmishes."

"But *we* won the seven before that."

Cudgel clenched his teeth. "We should settle this in single combat at dawn."

Carving Knife balled her fists. "Why wait till dawn?"

"Whoa—cool it, both of you," Dylan said. "You're brothers and sisters and you're all Maruunz. What's all the fighting about?"

The two Maruunz warriors explained that the woods around Nanni Town were dangerous, deep—and enchanted. Nothing ever aged there—not plants, not animals, and not humans. This had made a peculiar rite of passage possible. When Maruunz turned the age of thirteen, they were tested on their skills with their weapons. It was an important ritual because all Maruunz were called by the name of their weapon until they mastered it and were given a proper name. If they failed, they were cast unnamed and unaging into the woods until they were ready.

"Nanni once ruled this land," Cudgel said. "Then the Baron attacked. He couldn't find this hidden city, so he siphoned almost all the magic. That created the Dead Yard. Able-bodied Maruunz marched forth to fight him, but met their doom."

"I thought all the Maruunz were shadows," Ines said. "Why were you spared?"

"We were in the forests," Carving Knife responded. "That is where the Maruunz warriors train. The boys were learning their weapons, and the girls were mastering domestic skills. But now that we're at war, it makes sense for everybody to learn everything."

"So you weren't ready—all you guys are rejects?" Eli said.

"We've had four hundred years to hone our skills," Cudgel countered. "We are warriors—ready to take the Crimson Vision and claim our true names."

"You've been training for four hundred years?" Ines asked.

Cudgel shrugged. "Give or take a few decades. I kind of lost track about a century ago."

"We stayed to await our families' return," Carving Knife continued. "But over the years, our training exercises have become war. There have been losses on both sides."

"More losses on *your* side," Cudgel cracked.

"Can you keep quiet, even for a moment?" Carving Knife shot back.

"I'm speaking the truth—which is more than you usually do!" Cudgel roared.

Cudgel and Carving Knife stood face to face, breathing hard. The female Maruunz stood behind Carving Knife, weapons at the ready. The male Maruunz lined up behind Cudgel.

Dylan had seen this scene before, played out hundreds of times on the card table of his small apartment, in the backseat of the Professor's electric car, in the school hallway when he would brush by Viral Emma between periods.

Dylan stepped between the brothers and sisters. "Listen, I have a sister," he began. "The Baron may have her right now. I'm not certain exactly where he has her or how I can even get her back. I can't stop thinking about how pointless our fights were. You have another shot at being a family. Nanni went off to get your parents. They've been trapped in a shadow prison but she's going to free them and ask them to join an army to fight the Baron."

The Maruunz started to whistle and whoop.

"Then the prophecy is true," Cudgel said. "It has been said that Nanni will someday lead us in a war against an even greater foe."

"How many darn prophecies do you have on this island?" Eli asked no one in particular.

Cudgel led the children to a clearing in the shadow of the trees.

There, in an open pit, stood rows of statues. The figures, each of a Maruunz warrior, were exceedingly lifelike. They seemed less carved than frozen in place, suspended in a particular moment in time. Each statue was different—there were women and men, squat figures and tall ones, warriors bearing battle axes, and soldiers carrying slingshots. All had weapons of some sort and none of them was smiling. Dylan came closer to one. There was a hard proud look on his face and a scar on his left cheek.

"These statues seem almost alive," Ines said. "Who made them?"

"They are not statues," Cudgel said. "These are our parents. And our brothers and sisters, aunts and uncles. This is what is left of their bodies."

"I don't understand."

"Then we need to show you."

Cudgel, Carving Knife, and the other Maruunz turned their backs on Dylan and his friends. Together, side by side, their backs formed one big screen, and their moving tattoos leapt from one Maruunz to another. In silhouette, the tattoos were telling the story of the collective loss of their parents. Huge hummingbirds, clouding the sky, swooped down on warriors in a sneak attack. The Maruunz fought bravely, but were overwhelmed. Then, one by one, the birds reared back and plunged their beaks into the chests of their defeated foes, sucking the spirits out of them like nectar from a flower. Light flashed like paparazzi cameras as the shadows were loosed, and there was a puff of money-colored smoke. All that was left were rows of statues. The Maruunz kids turned back around, their faces grim.

"I thought when people lose their shadows, they eventually turn to dust or something," Eli said.

"It's the power of the forest," Carving Knife explained. "That's why Nanni sent the bodies back here. The same obeah that keeps us young preserves their forms. Not every spell has been sapped by the Baron."

"It just hit me," Ines said. "You said there's obeah released when shadows are stolen—and the Baron is hunting for more. So that's why the Baron is ripping people and their shadows apart! He's harvesting the magic!"

Dylan peered closer. None of the statues was casting a shadow.

"So why does the Baron need so much magic?" Ines asked.

"I wish I knew," Carving Knife said. "But it is said that the Baron has promised his people a return to the age before the Great Music, when birds ruled the earth and the air and their steps were thunder."

"Isn't that the way the rich always do us?" Eli seethed. "The shadows he's stealing—they're people's dreams! The Baron is taking the dreams of regular people to run his own schemes!"

"We will be hard-pressed if the Baron attacks again," Cudgel admitted. "We were once greater in number. Some of us left to join the crew of Ma Sinéad, the pirate queen."

"Ma Sinéad is a great female warrior," Carving Knife declared.

"Whatever," Cudgel mumbled.

"My sister loves pirates," Dylan said. "When this Ma Sinéad was here, did she say where she was going?"

Cudgel shrugged. "Ma Sinéad kind of does her own thing."

"Did she leave anything behind? A map? A note? A grocery list?"

"Only this moppet." Carving Knife pulled out a small figurine.

Dylan couldn't believe what he was seeing.

CHAPTER TWENTY-FIVE

Carving Knife was holding Emma's pirate doll!

"Y-y-you got that from Ma Sinéad?" Dylan asked.

That meant Emma wasn't a prisoner of the Baron. She was alive! But was she now a captive of the pirate queen?

Dylan snatched the doll away. That stupid thing had caused a lot of trouble, but he had never been happier to see it. "Tell me everything."

Carving Knife told Dylan that Ma Sinéad was a living legend. She was tall and dressed all in crimson, from her headscarf to her red leather boots. People thought she was only a myth up until a few months ago, when she had suddenly appeared and began to rally the people of Xamaica against the Baron.

She rode the wind in the *Black Starr*, her flying invisible ship. Her crew was stocked with outcasts—Iron Lions who didn't talk in questions, Higues with a thirst for adventure, and Wata Mamas with a hunger for action.

Ma Sinéad had come to Nanni Town just a short while ago on a recruiting mission—a Maruunz already in her crew had led her to the hidden city—and a number of the young Maruunz had joined her. Before Ma Sinéad left, she had bartered for food and supplies. She had traded the doll for coconuts from the great Palm of Protection, the milk of which is said to shield warriors in battle.

So Emma had probably joined up with Ma Sinéad. Or the pirate queen had captured her and ditched the doll. But Dylan didn't want to think about that, didn't want any more windows to fly open in his head. His heart pounded in his chest like it was trying to escape. He had to stay focused and positive.

"Was Ma Sinéad holding a little girl hostage?" Dylan asked.

"Cudgel and I were actually too busy fighting each other to notice," Carving Knife admitted.

"Nice. And you really have no idea where Ma Sinéad went?"

"When the big battle against the Baron comes," Carving Knife said, "she will no doubt be there."

Cudgel clapped his hands. "But why are we waiting around? Let us speak of happier things. You said Queen Nanni is off to free our people! We need to celebrate that!

Our new friends are right: let brother greet sister, and sister greet brother. Today we live—for tomorrow we die! It's time for us to return to our houses as one family and mark the occasion—Maruunz style!"

Was this guy crazy? With his sister possibly being held captive by friggin' pirates, Dylan definitely didn't feel like partying.

Carving Knife clapped him on the shoulder. "Don't you know the prophecy? The Great Web is falling! The Groundation nears its end! Tomorrow is the end of the world! What better reason to party?"

"One heart! One faith! Maruunz!" cried the Maruunz.

The wind passing through town was carrying the most delicious aromas Dylan had ever smelled. He couldn't identify the various scents—some were fragrant, some were tangy, others were sweet. The aromas seemed to have colors—green and red and yellow and golden-brown. Something delectable was being baked or stewed or roasted. Just by breathing in the wind, he could almost taste the flavor on his tongue and imagine the rich food in his mouth. Despite his bad mood, he was really hungry and he wondered what was cooking. They came to a wide, flat area in the center of town that was designated for public celebration. The Maruunz kids—boys and girls all working together—were laying out a feast. Hunters returned from the bush, bringing with them slain wild hogs. Cooks took the hog meat, cleaned it, carved it, and removed all the bones.

Dylan tried to keep his stomach from grumbling. "I am not in the mood for this."

"You're going to need your strength," Ines said. "If this is gonna be our final meal, let's make it a good one. Looks like they're making jerk!"

"You got in my face about eating with the plant people—but now you want to party with the Maruunz?"

"The Arrowaks turned out to be fireball-throwing zombies. The Maruunz are on our side. Big difference."

"It's not time for talking," one Maruunz said. "It's time for eating!"

Sitting down at a long mahogany banquet table, the kids started to eat. Dylan began with fruits, continued with several pieces of warm cassava bread, and finished with Maruunz-style jerk pork. It seemed impossible, but it tasted even better than it smelled—it was more than a taste, it engaged all your senses, filling you with visions and sounds of beautiful days and happy nights.

"Your food is even better than the Baron's nectar!" Eli remarked.

"It should be," Carving Knife boasted. "The Baron's beverage is brewed from stolen memories. He keeps them in his Green Cloud above his Golden Grove. Someday he'll likely sell us back our own thoughts, and the price will be blood."

"No wonder that nectar had such a bad aftertaste," Eli said.

The Maruunz kept bringing food. At some point Dylan held up his hands. "No more! I'm stuffed."

Several of the Maruunz began to dance. Dylan definitely was not in the mind-set for this. It was reminding him of how the whole disaster with the pirate doll and Viral Emma began.

Emma had won the state spelling bee and the science fair and some jealous jerk stole her pirate doll out of her locker as revenge. Dylan thought things were finally getting better at school when he and Eli got invited to a party—he and Eli were never on the guest list for parties. They snuck out before Emma could tag along. Turned out Chad was behind the party and it was being held at a friend's house whose parents were out. The party was pirate-themed and everyone was in costume. There was a talk-like-a-pirate contest and the prize was . . . Emma's stolen doll. The night only got worse after that. Dylan felt awful about the Viral Emma thing now. He had acted more like an other than a brother.

He tried to focus on the present. He realized he might be wrong about the Maruunz dancing—some of them were doing something more than that. At first Dylan thought they were performing this Brazilian fighting style he saw online once called capoeira—a couple of the movements seemed similar. But this was different. The dance was warlike—mixing punches and kicks with spins and thrusts. Dancers disappeared and reappeared, twisting about as lightly and easily as tendrils of smoke.

"This is the Bangaran fighting style," Carving Knife said proudly.

The kids watched in wonder. It was part martial arts, part choreography, part battle ritual, part celebration—and part magic. The movements of Bangaran were at the heart of the Maruunz approach to combat. Dylan had seen judo, karate, jiujitsu, and all sorts of martial arts on TV and in the movies—but he had never seen anything like this. He longed to learn more of its secrets. If he was going to find Emma—and maybe fight pirates or whomever—this was the kind of stuff he needed to know.

Then the drumbeat turned slower and the Maruunz started to sway to the rhythm. Nestuh creeped up closer to the gathering. Eli pointedly turned his back.

"Welcome back," Dylan said. "How're you doing?"

"I heard the drum, I had to come."

"What is it with spiders and drums?"

"The drum is the heartbeat of Xamaica," Nestuh explained. "Speaking of hearts, you should ask the girl to dance, mon."

"Ines? Are you kidding? We're from different worlds. Plus, she's an Iron Lion now."

"You got to keep an open mind in such things," Nestuh said. "I dated a caterpillar dis one time. She completely changed by the end of the relationship."

"Ines is totally older than me. She's like thirteen."

"I and I am 1,400 years old," Nestuh said. "But if a 700-year-old tarantula want to get all kissy-kissy, me not going to kick her off the web. Truth."

The drums really were hard to resist. Ines came over to Dylan. "Care to dance?"

"A girl asking Dylan to dance?" Eli chortled. "This really is the end of the world!"

Dylan wasn't going to do it, but Ines literally got her claws into him and pulled him onto the dance floor. She was still an Iron Lion, so Dylan held onto her furry neck. With his eyes closed, it was almost like he was dancing with a human girl. In fact . . .

"Ines, you're changing," Dylan said.

Ines kept swaying. "Looks like there's still some magic left in this town. Just keep dancing."

So for a moment they were a boy and girl, eyes closed, dancing to drums in the firelight.

"You know what I miss?" she said softly.

"What?"

"New Year's Day."

"How do you mean?"

"This celebration is giving me flashbacks. Back when I was a kid, my dad used to take me back to Seoul for the holidays to see some relatives. He'd let me dress up in a silk gown that belonged to his great-grandmother, and I'd wear these ceremonial hats and wooden sandals. I remember how the dress used to smell—all crisp and clean and ancient. It was like wearing a history book."

"That sounds great. In my house, New Year's Eve was for the birds. Literally."

"Not in Seoul. The whole neighborhood, the whole city for that matter, felt like my family. My dad would take me around to all the houses and I'd do this elaborate New Year's Day bow. I was beyond cute! Everyone would tuck a coin into my silk sashes. That's the custom. I made more money on New Year's Day than I made all year. It was the only time money ever meant anything to me." Ines put her head on Dylan's shoulder. "That was one of the last days my father and I spent real time together."

"But he's in all the Mee Corp. ads with you!"

"Most of those commercials we did—he wasn't even in the room. They use special effects to put him in the shots.

You can have a father and not have a dad." Ines brushed back the drape of black hair that hung over the right side of her face and wiped away a tear. "There must be some way for me to bring him back."

Dylan felt the curtain of depression coming down again. "I know how you feel. When you told me about my dad and how he died in that asylum . . ."

"I'm soooo sorry about that . . ."

"It's okay. It just feels like I'm a puzzle, and I'm missing a piece."

Later that night, everyone was woken up by a horrible rumble.

The Maruunz were already mustering. The kids and Nestuh gathered with them.

"The Baron cast a spell," Nestuh said. "The Palm of Protection has fallen."

"Impossible," Cudgel declared. "He'd need at least some general notion of where we are to send a spell. This city is still hidden."

"Did you cover your tracks when you returned from the forest?" asked Eli.

"We are warriors," Cudgel said, taking offense. "We have a code!"

"What he's trying to say is, no, we didn't," Carving Knife said. "We were too excited. We all thought our parents had come back."

"These really are the rejects," Eli whispered to Dylan. "I don't care that they've trained for four hundred years. The only thing seasoned around here is the food."

The ground shook again, and the palm trees swayed. A vast voice shook everything. It was the Grand Chirp.

"Now the time has come for the Bird Nation to collect its ancient inheritance!" the Baron announced in a disembodied voice. "We fight for all Xamaica! For what we do enriches us all!"

A Maruunz scout approached. "The Baron's army is nearing the city."

"What do we do now?" asked Ines, who had become an Iron Lion again.

"Resist!" Carving Knife and Cudgel shouted together.

"Dem finally have something to agree on," Nestuh sighed.

CHAPTER TWENTY-SIX

There was little time for the ordering of the battle.

Nanni Town was cannily constructed. Although it was a hidden city, it was also positioned to withstand a siege in case it was discovered. It was surrounded on two sides by rock walls and on the third by the river. That meant there was only one avenue into the city for invaders—through the forest.

Cudgel, Dylan, Eli, Ines, and Carving Knife huddled to discuss how to deploy their forces. They only had thirty-three people, counting Dylan and his friends. Who knew how many fighters the Baron had?

Dylan's heart was beating in his chest like a sneaker thumping in a dryer; his mind was racing NASCAR fast. *Focus*. The Professor had always told him that the ability to concentrate is a matter of life or death. She sure was right.

Nanni Town was a mess. The remains of the feast were scattered everywhere—half-filled pots, broken plates, and soup bones were strewn across the town. Maruunz warriors wandered about, looking for direction or their weapons. Dylan had to get it together if he was going to help put this ragtag group on track.

"So, we should decide on a battle plan," he announced. "Any ideas?"

"We spent four hundred years mastering our weapons," Cudgel said.

"What he means to say," Carving Knife clarified, "is that we didn't get around to overall combat strategy."

Eli looked grim. "Just shoot me now. Actually, the Baron will do it soon enough."

Nestuh was raising six of his eight legs.

"Yes?" Dylan said.

"I have a solution," Nestuh offered. "The Great Drum of Anancy."

"The what of who?" Eli asked.

"The Great Drum that rallied the beasts of Xamaica in the time of the Great Music!" Cudgel said. "If we had it we could bring all the creatures of the land to our side."

"Sounds like a plan," Dylan said. "Who has it, and where is it?"

"That's the problem," Cudgel said. "The Baron has the

drum. To get it, someone would have to sneak through his army, find his tent, and steal it."

Ines, Eli, and Dylan all shook their heads.

"Any other ideas that don't involve suicide missions?" Dylan asked.

"I need to do this, mon!" Nestuh pleaded. "All my life, all my 1,554 sisters—dem call me failure, now traitor, or even worse! I can't even spin a web. Truth. Let me do this one thing. I'm telling you, I never betrayed you! Let me prove I can do this."

"Nestuh, you don't have to prove—" began Ines.

"Oh yes he does," Eli cut in, flames rising from his horns.

"There's got to be another way," Dylan said. "You know the way you and Anjali took out Chad at school when I was on my skateboard and he was chasing me? We need to do something like that. Come out from unexpected places."

Dylan reasoned that the Baron hadn't found the exact location of the city yet, or else he would already be there. He had probably discovered some of the Maruunz's tracks and so he likely had a general idea where to look. That meant his army was probably broken up into different expeditionary parties. In the woods, there would be plenty of trees to conceal just how few in number the children were. They could pick apart the Baron's splintered forces group by group. That was Dylan's plan anyway.

Eli was sent to the river with the Maruunz boatmen. Perhaps their small fleet could lure the enemy and Eli, hiding by the bank, would also have the element of surprise.

Ines was dispatched above the town to lead the air assault. A couple Maruunz with long-distance weapons—

arrows, flying stars, and throwing axes—were placed under her command.

"I don't know if I can do this," Ines said. "This is a real battle."

Dylan put a hand on her furry feline shoulder. "You still think you're this little rich girl with a fake show?"

"I am. I'm a big faker."

"Listen, one time the Professor—I mean my aunt— she brought home this ostrich. It's like six feet tall. So of course it goes nuts and trashes the apartment. We thought it was gonna kill us. My aunt stays as cool as the other side of a pillow and gets it under control. So, do you know the difference between real courage and fake courage?"

"No, what?"

"Neither did the ostrich."

Dylan tried to look and sound sincere. He really meant what he was saying, even though he was mostly still thinking about his cheat code.

Ines smiled. "I almost forgot. I still have one thing left in my I-Got-Your-Back Pack."

"What?"

"I can't say. But when it's time to use it, you'll know. I gave some to Eli."

She handed him a small vial of a greenish-looking potion. He slipped it in his pocket and she flew off to her position.

Several minutes later, an argument broke out among some of the Maruunz. A few of the warriors were lobbying to fight on the front lines, but Cudgel would have none of it.

"What's going on?" Dylan interrupted.

"Well, they're Maruunz, but they're not really Maruunz,"

Cudgel explained. "We don't even let them train with us. They'd just hold everyone back."

"How bad could they be?"

"Dylan," Cudgel said, "meet Sharpened Stick, Piece of Rope, and Candle Holder."

"Did you really spend four hundred years training with a sharpened stick?" Dylan asked.

"Hey, we all had it better than Long Fingernails," said Sharpened Stick.

"Speak for yourself," said Sock Full of Flower Petals.

"I'm going to send this lot back to the village, out of the battle," Cudgel said, "given that their particular fields of weaponry are ridiculous."

"I don't know about that," Dylan said. "Back on Earth—I mean Babylon—I'm in class every day with guys just like this."

"I have a battle to wage," Cudgel declared, and he walked off. Nestuh gave Dylan an approving nod and skittered away too. Dylan stood in front of the rejects of the rejects.

Sharpened Stick, Piece of Rope, Candle Holder, and Sock Full of Flower Petals looked back at him with hope in their eyes and their almost certainly useless weapons in their hands. Dylan started chewing his nails. A feeling of hopelessness began to take over his brain like when you have ten seconds remaining in a test and twenty questions left. If he was ever going to find Emma, he had to lead these rejects to victory. But it seemed like whenever he tried to help his sister, he just ended up making things worse.

Like at that pirate party. Dylan had tried to take back Emma's stolen doll, but a dozen goons were ready to fight him for it. "Do the contest like everyone else," Chad had demanded. "Talk like Pirate Emma and we'll give you the doll." So Dylan did it: he gave a few "Ahoy, maties" and "Arggghs" and everyone laughed—until the girl in the pirate costume in the front row took off her mask. It was Emma, and she was crying. She grabbed the doll. "Argggh!" she screamed at the partygoers. "Are you entertained? Pirates don't even talk that way! That whole *argggh* thing got started in bad movies! Arrrrggggggghh!" The video Chad shot—*Pirate Girl Goes Crazy*—went viral. The nightmare only stopped after someone planted a virus on the clip and shut it down.

Dylan had to find someway to do something, but the trouble was, he didn't know anything. Then he thought about that guy—was his name Frantz Fanon?—that Emma used to quote: *What matters is not just to know the world but to change it.* Dylan didn't know how he was going to do that, but he had to try. He stopped biting his nails.

"Listen, guys," he announced, "you've been here for four hundred years. Time to grow up. Stay alert, and look to pitch in. Can you do that?"

Okay, it wasn't the best speech, but it was honest. And the rejects seemed to pick up on it. They saluted and scrambled to take up positions. Dylan armed himself with a rusty machete and caught up with Cudgel and the rest of the Maruunz in the forest. Maruunz specialized in concealing themselves before attacking. Even Dylan, who knew where to look, was surprised to see how well they blended in with the trees. He had twenty kids with him one second, and the next moment he was alone beneath a palm tree.

But the enemy did them one better.

CHAPTER TWENTY-SEVEN

Dylan couldn't see anyone else in the woods but he was not alone.

The forest smelled like new leaves. A powerful obeah had been cast here and he could feel it, like electricity running up and down his legs and arms. The magic had mostly been drained from Nanni Town, but amid the trees a natural mystic was circulating. Everything was young and fresh and growing. It was an invigorating environment. It was like coffee and a hot shower and an alarm clock all at once.

But something or somethings were tracking Dylan. He

could feel their hot gaze on his neck. A smell now hung in the air like the stench of dumpsters in summer. He began to walk faster—and then to run. He could see nothing, but he heard the stomp of feet, louder now, getting closer by the footfall. He looked around frantically for his comrades—but they were either too well hidden or gone. He wondered why no one saw him, why no Maruunz sprang to his aid. Where were they?

Then he halted.

That smell. The footfalls behind him. They weren't regular walking sounds. They were more like hops. Dylan drew his rusty machete—he had figured out what was on his trail. "Show yourselves!" he cried.

He spun around, stabbing wildly in the air. He struck something solid—a body?—and heard a roar that shook the trees and caused leaves to fall and flitter to the ground. Some of the leaves stopped in midair, balanced on the tops of the something or somethings.

Just then, Dylan's pursuers revealed themselves: he was surrounded by Hai-Uri.

Even in this strange land, they were weird creatures—one-sided, with one eye, one arm, one leg, and one sharp tooth in their mouth. Dylan hadn't seen them until they all turned around simultaneously. Now he was trapped in the center of a circle. And his friends wouldn't be able to rescue him: the backs of the Hai-Uri were invisible and so this whole attack wouldn't even be noticed from the other side.

The circle of Hai-Uri closed tighter and tighter around him. He could smell the breath of the beasts more strongly now—they reeked of rotten meat. Hungry tongues darted out of all the hungry mouths. He had to make a break for it.

Dylan figured that when a Hai-Uri's single eye was closed, it was essentially blind. The second he saw one blink, Dylan could run full force into it—and break out of the circle. The only problem with this plan: the creatures weren't blinking.

The circle closed and the single eyes continued staring straight ahead, toward the center, right into Dylan.

Something whispered through the air. One of the beasts stumbled, howling. A twig had stuck him right in his single eye. Sharpened Stick had saved him!

The creature blinked and Dylan burst through the constricting loop. Now he saw, all around him, that some of the Maruunz kids had been flushed out of hiding by the Hai-Uri. Their forces were scattered, and on the retreat. Dylan began to run as well.

He sprinted through the forest, knocking aside branches and vines. He jumped over streams and tripped on tree roots. Finally he came to the trunk of a hollow tree and he squeezed himself through a hole and covered it up behind him with a broad leaf.

He could hear the Hai-Uri passing by the trunk, invisible, hungry, looking for meat. He could hear their hops and pants and occasional roars. Then he heard something else in the dark of the tree trunk.

"It's me," came Carving Knife's voice.

Dylan's eyes adjusted. He could see her now.

"I guess we're screwed," Dylan said.

"How so? This is the most perfect day of my life," Carving Knife replied.

"Why?"

"There is no greater feat for a Maruunz than to be slain in battle. For us, a Death Day is even grander than a birthday."

"Happy, um, Death Day, I guess."

"A joke? This is no game, Babylonian."

"I never said—"

"I have heard that you and your friends believe this land is a game, like Shatranj. Trust me, if you die in Xamaica, you die. Some games you play. This game plays you." At that, Carving Knife buried her face in her hands.

"What's the matter? I thought Death Day was a good day!"

Carving Knife sniffled. "Yes, part of me longs for the heavenly hills of Zion. But there is something in me that wants to remain in the trees . . . never growing up . . . to stay with my brother always . . ." She wiped her eyes. "Anyway, I have a gift for you." She handed Dylan a club.

Dylan looked at her. "W-w-wasn't this Cudgel's weapon?"

"My brother was lucky—he has marched on to Zion."

A tattoo on her neck told the story—her brother had slain three Hai-Uri before being jumped by five more. Carving Knife finished off all the attackers—but too late.

"I have something for you." Dylan took out the potion Ines had given him. The vial said *Soon Come Serum* on the side.

"That's powerful obeah," Carving Knife said. "The element of surprise."

Dylan took a sip and offered the rest to her.

"Let us drink to my brother," she said, and then gulped the rest down. "Had he come of age, Cudgel would have taken the name Arianna."

"Really?"

"My brother was . . . complicated. Yes, we fought—but I guess that's why I loved him."

Dylan met Carving Knife's steady gaze. Her eyes had turned from black to red. The color had spread everywhere— the iris, the pupils, even the whites. It was a deep, natural red—like a ripe apple, or blood, or Mars on a clear night.

The Crimson Vision had come.

"So what should I call you?" Dylan asked.

"I name myself Astrid," she declared.

Astrid had come of age.

"One heart," Dylan said.

"One faith," Astrid answered.

"Maruunz!" they said together.

They burst out of the tree trunk. At that moment, Dylan heard a cry from above—it was Ines, swooping down. She roared—and her roar was louder than the cry of the Hai-Uri. It shook the tree trunks, and caused some to topple, tearing from the earth, roots and all. Her war-roar echoed across the sky and caused the ground to rumble and shake. They had taken the Hai-Uri by surprise.

"Drive them to the river!" Ines shouted.

The Maruunz closed ranks and Dylan and Ines hurried over to join them. The hunted were now the hunters. Startled, some of the Hai-Uri turned and broke ranks. Once the creatures began to move, they were no longer invisible. The Maruunz warriors started to run after them.

"Maruunz—rally to me!" Astrid shouted.

The Hai-Uri began to hop and stumble. Ines roared again and now the creatures began to flee wildly. The Maruunz ran after them in pursuit. Dylan swung his borrowed weapon wildly, taking two Hai-Uri out and forcing others to retreat.

The Hai-Uri hopped quickly, but the Maruunz knew the forest. They dodged the branches, sprang over tree roots, swung on vines, and kept hot on the heels—or heel—of their prey. Many of the monsters tripped and fell. Piece of Rope had booby-trapped the forest floor!

In a flash the Maruunz warriors were on the fallen creatures. With spinning Bangaran kicks and punches they subdued them. The remaining Hai-Uri kept fleeing toward the river. Dylan dropped the club, drew his rusty machete, and followed.

Eli was waiting by the riverbank. There were dry leaves there, as things aged and died normally outside of the enchantment of the forest. Eli breathed fire and set the leaves ablaze like kindling as the Hai-Uri approached. The Hai-Uri, stunned and fearful, threw themselves into the river to escape being burned. As it turned out, one-legged creatures are even worse at swimming than they are at running. They quickly sank beneath the surface. This was turning into a one-sided battle.

Eli raced away from the river and, along with Nestuh, pursued some of the Hai-Uri out through a grove of trees back in the direction from which they had come. Their opponents were in full retreat. Candle Holder had spread oil over the water—he then set it ablaze with a lit candle! None of the Hai-Uri surfaced.

Ines spread her iron wings and roared, "Victory!"

Dylan walked up to Piece of Rope, Candle Holder, Sharpened Stick, and Sock Full of Flower Petals. He slid his rusty machete back in his belt loop. "I have to admit, you guys were pretty helpful," he said.

"I guess four hundred years of puberty is plenty," Sharpened Stick remarked. "Besides, it was Sock's idea!"

Sock Full of Flower Petals was tossing some of the contents of his sock into the air in celebration.

"It's too early to start throwing a jubilee," Astrid warned. "That was just a scouting party. And now the Baron knows exactly where we are."

"We need another plan. Where are Eli and Nestuh?"

No sooner had Dylan asked this question when he heard someone sobbing in the forest. He and Ines ran over to look. They spotted Eli—his huge Rolling Calf body was slumped in a grove of trees near the riverbank. Rivulets of flame ran up and down his flanks. He was weeping, but his tears turned to steam and floated up his cheek, rising past his horns, up into the sky, where they evaporated in the warm Xamaican sun.

"What happened?" Dylan asked.

"I was fighting alongside Nestuh," Eli said, waving some of the steam away from his face. "We had driven them back. Then he said something about getting the drum."

"The Great Drum of Anancy?" Ines said. "Did he try to go and get it? That's suicide!"

"Why didn't you stop him?" Dylan asked.

"I followed him for a bit, helped him break through the lines. We had them on the run. But my Soon Come Serum wore off. And I . . . I . . . got sidetracked."

"Nanni's book," Dylan said.

Dylan could see now that Eli was clutching the book

to his smoldering chest. Dylan pulled it away from him in disgust and tossed it at the feet of a Maruunz warrior.

"It was like the Baron was in my head tempting me!" Eli sobbed. "I felt this . . . this greed. The Baron's men had taken the book. I tried to take it back."

"We don't need the book," Ines said.

"I have bills to pay. Don't you remember what the Soucouyant showed us? My family is gonna get ripped apart unless I come home with some money!"

"That was an illusion," Dylan said.

"It felt real to me! My family has spent their life savings taking care of me. I need that book. The wealth of the world! It could make this whole stinking trip worth it!"

"So that's why you left Nestuh?" Ines began crying; tears streamed down her Iron Lion face. "For money?"

"It was only gonna take a second to get it! But after I turned away, that's when the ambush hit. Higues everywhere. And Soucouyants too."

Ines and Dylan looked at Eli in disbelief.

"They got him," Eli cried. "He's gone."

BOOK FOUR

GROUNDATION: THE FINAL BATTLE

CHAPTER TWENTY-EIGHT

The Baron had captured Nestuh. Three days were up. Morning had slithered into the sky and there were two moons hanging above the clouds. There was also Earth itself, looming above, bright and blue. Xamaica and the Earth seemed to be on a collision course. The sky was undone and the Groundation was nearly complete. The Great Web of the World was hanging by a single strand. Equality, Liberty, and Vitality had come untethered. Only Mystery remained. The Great Web hung on that last principle, flapping like a flag in the wind. And Nestuh was gone.

"He wanted that drum in the worst way," Eli sobbed.

"He said it was the only way we were gonna win. I drove him to it. I get it! I screwed up!"

The Baron's forces marched on. From the West came the great dragons—of air, of fire, and, swimming down the Black River, of water. They spurted flame and blackened the earth and churned the water and darkened the sky with smoke as they made their way toward the battleground.

The Baron's forces marched on. From the South came the Soucouyants and all manner of creatures that terrified and haunted. They came entwined with legions of zombies. The Soucouyants' shrieking voices taunted their enemies and their Venus flytrap hands cradled deadly fireballs.

The Baron's forces marched on. From the East came the Iron Lions, and each one carried a golden spear and a golden shield and wore a golden helmet. And from the North came the hummingbirds, and when the children saw them, their hearts sank. They were no longer birds, but something older, something ancient—the beasts they had been before the Great Music. By some obeah, they had sharper beaks and longer talons and leather wings. The hulking warrior beasts closest to the Baron boasted low numbers on their chests—5, 4, 3, and 2. The Baron himself—familiar in a much larger version of his tattered top hat—flew before them. His gold 1 glowed brighter than ever, and he unleashed a cry louder by far than the Grand Chirp.

The Baron was no longer shorter than this sentence. He was bigger than this book, larger than a library, gigantic and bloated and terrible. His eyes were menacing and unblinking, his wings were like those of a vast bat, and his beak was filled with cruel teeth, each one the size of a small child.

Around his mouth, like a squid, were a tangle of tentacles, thrashing, squirming, covered with suckers. He was no tiny creature one had to strain to hear and see. He had taken the form of a massive primeval beast, mottled with slimy scales and long crimson feathers, neither fish nor fowl, but clearly very fishy and definitely really foul.

Dylan's double scratches felt like squirming snakes, lashing and biting his chest and filling it with icy venom. Now he knew for sure how he had gotten them—the Baron had done it. He could feel the connection. Even when Dylan was playing the game, the Baron had been reaching across worlds, trying to destroy him. A cold rage built up inside Dylan. He knew enough about ornithology to know that dinosaurs and birds were part of the same prehistoric family. "Did you know some dinosaurs had feathers?" the Professor would say excitedly. "Did you know they sat on their eggs just like birds? Dinosaurs never died—they're in the skies!" And she was right. Whatever thing the Baron had transmogrified into was a huge horrid relative of birds, a missing link to the beasts of the sea, and a rude, distant cousin of dinosaurs. But this was the crazy uncle that never got invited to the family reunions.

"No wonder the Professor was a bird watcher," Dylan murmured. "The tranquilizers. The heavy rope. The shark cage. This is the thing she was watching for."

The Baron's bulk blotted out the sun, the Earth, and both moons. Over him hung the Green Cloud, milked from a million memories, turning any light that was left the color of commerce. Around him swarmed the Higues, their awful insect wings buzzing, their gray hoods thrown back, their horrible proboscises exposed and extended and dripping blood. In one clawed hand, the Baron held the Great Drum and he beat a rhythm that mesmerized the others and drew them to him. *Doom, Doom, Doom* went the Great Drum—on and on until it beat ninety-nine times.

"Now we know why the Baron called the Green Cloud intellectual property," Eli said.

"Yeah—anyone with an intellect is the Baron's property!" Ines replied.

The Baron's hoards had raised their voices in song, which sounded like a pack of wolves howling the notes to "Ride of the Valkyries."

Blood and treasure
Blood and treasure
Blood and treasure
Jah is dead

Nearby, on a moving cart, Nestuh was tied down with ropes, a prisoner of the Baron.

"This is my fault," Eli moaned. "I wanted that treasure. I got so fixated on one direction I completely lost my way."

"There has to be some way of reaching him!" Ines said.

"We'd need an army to do that," Dylan said.

"We'd need a miracle to do that," Eli added.

A large shadow suddenly fell across the field of battle. It was huge, and it soon became apparent that it was made up of many smaller shadows, shadows of men and women. They stood straight and tall and proud and they had weapons in their hands. They wielded machetes and spears and bows and maces. Each shadow began to take shape. The darkness became flesh, the flesh became warriors. Their eyes burned red. The warriors were Maruunz.

The shadowless statues had been made human again. One thought had kept them: *Family*. Nanni had razed the walls of the shadow prison, and now she had raised an army.

Nanni stood at the top of Pumpkin Hill and the children stood with her. She put her lips to the abeng and blew a single loud note. For a brief moment, a cool shadow of calm was cast over the land. But still the legions of the Baron trudged on.

"I didn't know there were this many creatures in all of Xamaica," Dylan said.

"There aren't," Eli announced. "I just figured it out. Some of the Baron's army is made up of the avatars of kids who play Xamaica on Earth."

Ines looked stricken. "My global friends—Artur and the rest!"

"Now the Baron has snared them all," Eli said.

Behind the Baron's forces was his spinning castle, perched upon its familiar funnel cloud. He had brought the tornado tower with him to watch the war. No doubt the inhabitants were wagering heavily on the outcome of the battle. Nearby, there were lines of empty wooden carts, each flanked by winged dinosaur guards.

Dylan shook his head. "Wishcoins! They think war's gonna make them rich."

Dylan had never wanted his powers to work more than he did in that moment. That feathered thing was the source of his family's suffering. That monster stood between him and his sister. With all that was in him, he wanted to strike it down. In the game he had been a force to reckon with. Now, this was no game and he needed all the strength he'd once had. He had hoped that something would trigger it—the Xamaican sun, the Xamaican sea, the Xamaican earth. He had hoped that the danger would set off a reflex. Nothing. He had nothing. He was powerless.

Then the Baron laughed—and the sound was like shells rattling in a burlap bag. A chill descended. The Baron put down the Great Drum and motioned with a talon. Nestuh was brought forward, each of his eight arms tied with rope to a wooden cart. Four monstrous dinosaur guards surrounded him.

They were going to rip off Nestuh's limbs.

"I'm good, mon!" Nestuh cried out to the kids. "I have eight legs! If I lose a few, I'll just be like Eli! Do they make wheelie chairs for spiders?"

Then Nestuh let loose an awful shriek as a guard pulled off one of his legs.

"Nooo!" Ines screamed. "We have to stop this!"

(Leave the spider) Nanni said to the Baron and his men. Her voice was so full of cold command, for a second it seemed the Baron's men would stop.

"Obey *me* and you'll be rewarded!" the Baron roared. He motioned for the imaginary wishcoins to be thrown from the carts to the troops, who grabbed at the air.

He signaled again. Another awful cry. Another leg was ripped off Nestuh.

"That evil coward!" Ines groaned, tears in her eyes.

(No one is good or evil. Never demonize any person or any thing. There is only this moment, and a choice)

The guards were readying to pull off one more limb.

"Don't give in!" the spider shouted to the children. "I'm done for anyway, mon!"

"We have to do something!" Eli cried.

Another leg was pulled off. Nestuh had stopped joking, talking, or even moving. He was clearly in incredible pain. Dylan couldn't just stand and watch. He began to run toward the cart where Nestuh was being held. Ines and Eli followed right after him.

(No) Nanni said, and set a restraining hand on Dylan's shoulder.

The day was hot, there was no wind, and the air was thick with fear. Nanni's eyes were sad but calm.

"We have to save him," Dylan pleaded.

Nanni turned to her Maruunz commanders. Astrid, her red eyes shining, stepped forward. Now that she was a full Maruunz warrior, she had been placed in charge of the forward forces. Tattoos on her neck, arms, and legs told of her most recent exploits, including a skirmish with hummingbirds, a close call with a Higue, a full-on fight with Soucouyants. Her chief lieutenant was Sharpened Stick, whose eyes were also blazing crimson, for he too had come of age and taken the name of Obadiah. Instead of his old namesake weapon, he was literally carrying a very big stick: Cudgel's club.

"Nestuh is being held in the center of the Baron's armies," Astrid reported in a steady voice that showed she was ready for leadership. "Even with our reinforcements, he has, by far, the superior numbers."

With the tip of a knife, she drew a map in the red earth.

"If we launch an incursion, we will be flanked by dragons on the left and Iron Lions on the right. We'll have trouble enough dealing with the Soucouyants, Hai-Uri, and Higues in the center. If the Rolling Calves charge they'll roll right over us."

(So it's a trap. What is your counsel?)

"The Baron means to draw us in and finish us," Astrid reasoned. "My Queen, you know these mountains like you know your own mind. If we retreat, the Baron will not be able to stop us. We can harass his forces for years—centuries . . ."

Nestuh's howls again echoed through the canopy.

"We're going after Nestuh," Dylan declared.

Eli and Ines, with Dylan by their side, turned to head toward the front lines.

(No!) Nanni rose up, tall as a tree, her eyes flashing. (Don't be a fool! If you lead forces into the Baron's trap, we will lose this war. You will obey me!)

"Or what?" Dylan countered. "I thought you changed! But it's still your way or nothing! You're still a tyrant!"

(Do not disobey me. We are outnumbered. We must fight together or fall together)

"What about Nestuh?"

(We're at war. He is not our problem)

Dylan looked her in the eyes. "He's not our *problem*, he's our *friend*. We're not gonna let you sacrifice him like some piece in a game. If you can't understand, maybe you haven't changed. We're the Game Changers, all of us! This is about friendship."

(What do you all know about that?) she spat. (I know your hearts)

"You don't know anything about us," Ines said.

(Silence, brat. I know everything. Everything! You came here to save your dear old dad. You failed and now he's gone from this world. He was a fraud—and so are you)

"You're wrong," Ines said, her cat's eyes brimming with tears. "My show was fake, but every adventure I've had here is real. And I believe in my dad, I don't care what anybody says. One thing I've figured out is if you believe in something enough—even yourself—you can make it real."

"She's answered you, witch," Eli said. "Now leave her alone!"

(Shut up, fool!) Nanni sneered, turning to Eli. (Your illness is tearing your family apart. And now your lust for treasure has condemned Nestuh to death. You should be ashamed!)

"Yeah, I screwed up big-time," Eli admitted. "But I know now there are things worth more than money. I'm not going to leave Nestuh again."

"Queen Nanni, you've said enough," Dylan said.

(Have I? I can read your thoughts like words on a page. You came here to find your sister. But you're the one that lost her, aren't you? You've always been jealous of her intelligence, her talent, her height. So you insulted her—and now you have sent her to her doom. The question isn't how you will live without your sister. It's how you will manage to live with yourself)

Fury swelled up in Dylan. But she was right—this trip, this war, Nestuh's capture, they were all his fault. He was a jealous jerk of a brother and it took this whole journey and a friggin' war for him to see it. He wanted to attack Nanni for saying any of this out loud. But that was exactly what she wanted, right? For the kids to lose control, to forget the real mission—freeing Nestuh and then finding his sister. He had to simmer down, to focus. He had to be calm for his friend—for Nestuh. So Dylan swallowed his rage and stayed silent.

Nanni laughed. (Are you listening to my words? Or are you too sick with your own guiltiness? I am the Mistress of the Maruunz! Sorceress of the Land of Look Behind! The Queen of the Dark Interval! How dare you lecture me about sacrifice and responsibility—my blood is in the soil of this land! You're not here to serve ideals. You're here for yourselves! I know your family history! I can read your minds like . . . like—)

Her words caught in her throat. It was as if her mental powers had encountered something unexpected in Dylan's thoughts. For a moment Nanni's face was full of anger and pain. Centuries were etched around her eyes.

Then she seemed to shrink. A sad look passed over her face, a breeze rippling across the open waters, and then her expression was one of stillness again. She bowed her head, overcome by some thought or emotion.

Dylan's own anger subsided, and he looked at the witch with pity. "Whatever we came for, we're here for each other now. This is about friendship. But you wouldn't know anything about that, would you? We've heard stories about you since we got here and all of them are bad. And you seem to live up to every terrible word. That why I don't believe you've really changed. You're still the same cruel, thoughtless witch you've always been!"

A silence hung over the group for a moment, but it was broken by another scream from Nestuh. Then Nanni spoke.

(You think you know me, but you know nothing. I've been to your world. I've felt different feelings—happiness, friendship . . . even love. That's where I changed. If only I could bring those days back . . . bring those feelings back. If only . . . for a time)

She now looked like the old woman she was, shriveled and stooped over and unimaginably exhausted. She could read the thoughts of others, but now it seemed that the others could finally read hers. Her life had been long and heavy and cold. The children's desires were small and desperate but they burned as bright as a star. Something like a smile fluttered around her lips, but it was drowned by the melancholy in her voice.

(By Jah, I have changed) she said. (Nestuh came to my aid when others gave me up for dead. He was my friend because he sensed something worthy in me. So I will be his friend now. Let us come to his aid. Let us rescue . . . our friend)

Suddenly she was a commander again, standing straight with renewed energy. She faced Astrid.

(Is there any chance our attack will succeed?)

Astrid shook her head. "Your Majesty, we are certain to fail."

Nanni turned to Dylan and her lieutenants. (By the Inklings, if you heed one thing I say, remember this. The only defeat is when you quit)

CHAPTER TWENTY-NINE

Nanni motioned Dylan to come away from the others and walk with her.

"We don't have time for more meetings!"

(There is always time to do things right)

Nanni and Dylan walked together, much as they had the first day they met when they had toured Nanni Town. They strolled to the crest of a grassy knoll and peered down at the battlefield. Flowers dappled the grass. Dylan could hear the echoes of battle preparations: the screech of swords being sharpened, the grunts of marching soldiers, and the stomp of armored feet. The long grass and flowers waved blithely in the breeze.

"Why are you showing me this?" Dylan asked impatiently. "We have to help Nestuh!"

(Those purple blossoms are called Lovelies of the Forest. Xamaica has many flowers, but I never paused to pick one until I strolled through a field of dandelions on Earth)

"Flowers? Seriously? This is what you want to talk about?"

(I sense great turmoil in you)

"I get that a lot. I just want to hurry up already. We have a war to win!"

(How many battles have you fought?)

"Not counting the one earlier today? Between not many and none. How about you?"

(Too many to count—here and on Earth)

"So you were trying to conquer Earth too?"

(A score of years ago, I was searching for fresh sources of obeah. A human digging for prehistorical beasts disrupted the skein between the worlds—and I broke through)

"So why didn't you end up ruling a couple continents?"

(Love)

"Excuse me, did you say *love*?"

(He was extraordinary. I don't know if he ever completely believed my stories about Xamaica, but he wrote them down and said someday he'd share them with the world)

"So love is why you never conquered Earth?"

(In battle, the victory goes to the one who knows how to yield. When I play Shatranj, I keep my mind open and surrender to the moment)

"I don't understand."

(Don't understand. *Over*stand)

"Enough with the wordplay. What are we going to do about this war?"

(The Way is all around you. But you can only find it within yourself)

"Since when did you become this philosopher?"

(After I spent time in your world, I returned to my own but remained lost. I learned that the Baron had been corrupted by his pursuit of me, and was now dedicated to increasing his own power. I found myself listening to the thoughts of Xamaicans. I safeguarded their greatest treasures in my magic book)

"My sister likes collecting things in books too. You two have a lot in common. Except she's not magic or evil or two thousand years old . . . So is there anything you can tell me that I can actually use in the battle so I don't get, y'know, killed?"

(I have lived all these long centuries because my magic protects only me. I have perfected the art of self-defense. Friendship, family—these things leave one vulnerable, weak)

"So that's a no?"

Nanni struck a pose, her legs slightly bent, her arms out in front of her.

(Do what I do)

"This is not the time for choreography."

(This is the first position of Bangaran—it's called the backward hummingbird)

"Oh—my bad. This is actual battle stuff. Now I get it." Dylan tried it out. It felt unexpectedly natural; he could feel a winged energy flowing through him, like he had been plugged into a socket. "Cool!"

She shifted positions. (This is the resting dragonfly—the second position)

Dylan adjusted his stance. He felt a flow of power, but this time it was different—it was the calm force of a slow-moving flood.

(And this is the swaying palm tree—the third position)

Dylan changed his stance again. With this new position, he felt like he had captured a whirlwind in his body. His skin tingled and his muscles throbbed. "The power—it's incredible."

Nanni smiled. (Good—you have natural aptitude for Bangaran)

"Will this help me in a fight?"

(Yes—if we had seven years to train)

"How about something that will come in handy in seven minutes?"

Nanni waved her hands. A machete appeared in front of her. Flames ran up and down the blade.

"What's that?" Dylan said.

(It is the Machete of the Land of Look Behind. I forged this blade when I was exiled to the wilderness many ages ago. I was alone and frightened and I drew energy from my own spirit. Courage ignites it. As long as there is bravery in your heart, flames will run on this blade, burning all enemies)

"I could use an upgrade," Dylan said, pulling his rusty machete out of his belt loop and dropping it on the ground. When he grabbed the hilt of the new weapon, the fire went out. "I'm guessing this is not a good sign."

(When the flames return, you'll be ready)

Dylan smiled. "If you're not careful, we're going to become friends."

Nanni put a hand on his shoulder. (Friendship can be relative)

CHAPTER THIRTY

After everything they'd already been through, Dylan couldn't believe it was going to end like this.

He looked out again across the field of battle. The Baron's forces had dug into their positions. The flowers he had admired only moments ago had been trampled. Spread out over the vast square, he saw fiends from beyond his nightmares. There were creatures with claws and horns and forked tongues. There were beasts with cruel eyes and terrible voices and deadly weapons. There were wild things that he wouldn't have dared to imagine, and yet here they were, real and thirsty for blood.

And the most terrifying one of them all was coming right for him.

The Baron.

Even from a distance he could feel the sinister intent of the Crimson Beast. Through the failing light of day, he could see its eyes burning bright. The cavern of its mouth was filled with the stalagmites and stalactites of its teeth. Its bulky form towered above the landscape. Its wings, feathered like a crow's in some places, naked like a bat's in others, spread out wider than the branches of tall trees.

The two scratches across Dylan's chest felt like they were splitting open. A chill ran through him. He put his hand to his heart—he could hear the Baron in his mind.

Leave this place.

Heck to the no.

What if all of this isn't real? What if it's a dream?

It is real . . . Why wouldn't it be?

Remember your condition? The one that you won't discuss with anyone, not even your best friend? Yes—you had another seizure. The game set it off. Your eyes rolled into the back of your head. Your limbs flailed like a drowning boy. You swallowed your tongue. You nearly died.

Stop it.

Video games trigger your seizures. And it's happening again. You never made it to the Mee Mansion. You never entered the Tournament of Xamaica. You never left the nurse's office! Where do you think those gashes in your chest came from? In your confusion you tried to tear out your own heart! Playing Xamaica triggered a massive seizure. Just like the doctor told you it would.

That's not true.

King Games is dying! But it's not too late to save yourself, to make your exodus. Remember Hope Road? You get three trips. You have one left. Close your eyes. Think of home. The path will appear. With a single step, you will leave your friends behind and the road will take you where you need to go. All this death will vanish like a dream. But if you insist on believing in this world, if you keep fighting for your friends, you will die. You will choke on your tongue. The seizure will kill you.

Images entered Dylan's mind.

He was lying on the floor of the nurse's office. Emma was there too. She was begging Dylan to get up, stand up, to leave whatever fantasy had gripped his conscious mind and come back to the real world.

No.

His real sister was still out there somewhere. If he was ever going to find her, he had to win this battle. The nurse's office vanished.

You can't win! You failed to discover the spell that can restore your powers. I know that secret. I've found the greatest source of magic: Greed! *It is inevitable, inexhaustible, irresistible. We can create a new kingdom powered by greed.*

"I'd rather destroy you than join you."

You have no powers. I know about the cheat code. I know that it is your own name.

"H-h-how did you find that out?"

This is my world—I know all! This isn't your place. This isn't your problem!

"I don't run from problems. Not anymore."

Dylan was going to find his sister no matter what. Emma was a pain, yes, but they had always been there for each other. He missed her worse than he thought he could ever miss anything.

Suddenly Ines and Eli were standing beside him. But the Baron wasn't finished yet.

Ines! Your father is gone, but I can make you queen of this world. With my Green Cloud you could live the fantasies of every Xamaican, and we could drain the dreams of Earth as well! You can be a monarch greater than any tale told on TV or in movies!

"I don't believe you," Ines said. "And I believe my father is still out there, somewhere. I don't need empty fantasies or reality TV. I'll bring Dad back without you."

Eli—fight beside me! I can give you all the wealth in this world. I can give you Nanni's book!

Eli laughed. "Don't you get it? We're the Game Changers! A true player knows when they're being played!"

Then—Game Changers—prepare to meet your fate.

And just like that, the Baron vanished from their minds.

Dylan and his friends were back on the battlefield. Dylan felt his heart falter, and his stomach go jumpy. He turned to his friends. "I'm sorry."

"For what?" Eli asked.

"For everything. For bringing you here."

Ines struck him in the shoulder with her paw, not enough to knock him down, but hard enough to get his attention. "Don't you know by now that, for us, the only place to be is where you are? Besides, it's my fault too. Greatest. Adventure. Ever. Remember?"

"I gotta admit, hanging with you hasn't been so bad," Eli

said to her. "When we started, I thought you were a shallow, empty-headed, corporate tool with a mean streak. Now I know you don't have a mean streak."

Ines flicked at Eli with her tail. The two kids exchanged smiles. But they no doubt knew, as Dylan did, that there was no hope.

"So, what's your plan?" Ines asked Eli.

"This time," Eli admitted, "I don't have one."

"Well, I do," Dylan said. "You ever wonder why the Baron didn't attack us at the Tournament of Xamaica?"

"I assume he was watching us, studying our moves."

"So he's gonna expect us to do what we did then. Stick together, work as a team."

"So we should do the opposite," Eli said. "Spread out. Each take command of a separate part of the army."

"Why would they let us command anything?" Ines asked.

"Nobody here knows that we don't know anything," Dylan said. "And aren't you an expert at pretending you know what you're doing?"

Ines clapped her paws. "Neither does the ostrich!"

"The crazy thing is what she just said makes sense to me," Eli said.

They quickly sketched out battle plans. This was the end of all things, but they were together, at least for now.

"One heart," Ines said, lightly touching Dylan's shoulder this time.

"One faith," Eli chimed in.

"Group hug?" Ines suggested.

"I have to tell you something," Dylan confessed. "When we played the game—I used a cheat code. It enhanced my powers."

Ines smiled. "Yeah—it's in your file. That isn't the only reason you're good. Your name is part of the code of this world—don't you think that's a sign you're special?"

"I knew about it too," Eli admitted. "Since when is hacking cheating? You won't get out of the group hug that easily."

The children embraced for a bit, and then moved on.

Dylan looked out across the battlefield. There was smoke, fire, flying creatures, slithering monsters, marching armies, roars and commands, sunlight glinting off weaponry, arrows flying through the sky. So much chaos. How would he find his own way, much less lead others into battle?

He thought about Emma. She'd probably have a quote for this, maybe something by that poet Claude McKay, the one about being surrounded and outnumbered and fighting back anyway.

Yes, they were going to die. Dylan couldn't understand how it had come to this.

He stopped walking. He had to *overstand*. He closed his eyes, cleared his thoughts.

In his mind's eye, the battlefield became a chessboard, with rows and columns. Where there had been chaos, there was now order. He could see where he had to go and what he had to do. He opened his eyes, drew his machete—and flames ran up the blade.

His friends by his side, Dylan prepared for the final charge.

Nanni anchored the center, Astrid led the left, and the kids—Dylan, Eli, and Ines—spread out across the forces on the right.

When Astrid raised the standard of the Maruunz, a blood-red flag, fair and bold, Nanni conjured explosions of light that appeared to blind their opponents. The Baron's forces melted before the onslaught of the Maruunz, and for a moment there was hope.

Dylan and his friends—keeping plenty of space between them—waded through the lines of Hai-Uri. Nanni threw lightning bolts that gave cover to their attack. The monsters fell back, howling, and the Baron's army seemed in disarray.

Nanni's attack was something to behold. She held no weapons, and she carried no shield. Her body undulated and her arms waved like smoke in the wind. This was Bangaran, mastered at its highest level. She appeared to one and all like a tongue of fire, bright and terrible. Men and creatures threw themselves upon her and fell back, singed and burned or utterly consumed by some magic conflagration.

But the center held. For it was here, around the captured Nestuh, that the Baron had concentrated his best fighters— the Iron Lions and the Soucouyants, the zombies and his imperial bird-dinosaur guard. From above came swarms of Higues, flying on their mosquito wings, their hoods thrown back to reveal their bulbous red eyes. Each carried a shield and a crooked dagger; and each had a proboscis that was already dripping with newly-tasted blood. There were hundreds of them, thick as insects over a fetid pond. The sound of their coming filled the air with a sharp wild buzzing that stung the ears and made the heart grow weak.

Nanni, however, brushed them off like, well, insects, swatting and swaying and unconquered on the piece of land she had claimed for her own.

But then, from the sides, came phalanxes of Rolling Calves. When they charged into Nanni, the sound was like a landslide. But still she resisted, using her Bangaran skills to throw them back, their fires extinguished, ashes everywhere.

On another part of the battlefield, Dylan was under attack. The Baron had dispatched the Soucouyants to ambush him. The creatures sent vinelike creepers to trip up the Maruunz warriors around Dylan and threw fireballs to finish them off. He dodged a few of them, unconsciously using some of the basic Bangaran moves Nanni had taught him. With his machete, he repelled a dozen more attackers, who retreated in fear at the sight of his flaming blade. But a fresh wave of Soucouyants continued the attack. Any moment now and they would be on top of Dylan and burn him alive. They screeched at him with their terrible chilly voices.

"Dylan needs our help!" Ines cried out from across the battlefield. "I'm not gonna get there in time!"

Eli was held up, many paces away, in a skirmish with the Higues. "Hold on!"

The Soucouyants opened their Venus flytrap hands, which immediately filled with deadly flames.

(No!)

Nanni summoned up deep reserves of obeah to blow out the flames of the Soucouyants and knock them back. Taken by surprise by Nanni's defense of Dylan, some of the Soucouyants were finished off by the Maruunz, who suddenly had the upper hand. Dylan dispatched the stragglers with his flaming machete. The attack, however, took its toll on Nanni. Her face aged, her back bent, and her flame withered.

Now the Baron sprung his most fearsome trap. He had been waiting for the witch to divert her magic to help her friends—for then she would be at her weakest. Right at Nanni's feet, the ground gave way and her concentration, for a brief moment, was broken. Beneath her swarmed all manner of horrible, gigantic worms—brown and black, crimson and emerald, golden and gray. They threw off a great heat, as if the ground had opened up into hell itself. These unexpected monsters were the dragons of earth, tamed by some mighty spell and compelled to follow the Baron's bidding. The huge worms wrapped around Nanni's arms and legs and waist and soon she was immobilized.

Nanni was a prisoner.

CHAPTER THIRTY-ONE

Two feathered dinosaurs, croaking with glee, clamped manacles on Nanni and flew her to the Baron. Before, he could imprison her, but not slay her, because the enchantment around her was too powerful. Now, with so much of her power dispersed to protect her allies, she was, at long last, vulnerable to attack. His centuries-long wait was over.

Finally, the Baron gloated, *my victory is complete. I name myself Emperor Zarathustra I! The Great Web of the World will fall—and I will build an infinitely superior enclosure. The Grand Birdcage of Zarathustra—or so future generations shall call it—will cover Xamaica and Earth. I'm sick of sipping nectar. From this day on I'll eat as other birds do—and all the people of two worlds will be worms!*

There were so many crazy things going on in that speech, Dylan didn't know where to begin. A giant birdcage? Two planets full of worms? That last idea in particular overwhelmed Dylan's mind as he tried to imagine it. Every kid in his school—worms. Both houses of Congress—worms. All the actors and actresses at the Oscars—all worms. Okay, maybe the members of Congress and the actors and some of the kids in school deserved it, but what about all the poets and philosophers and skateboarders and doctors? How sick would it be to see city streets filled with a traffic jam of human-sized worms, or a river of worms slithering through malls and multiplexes and up and down the Washington Monument? It was too awful to think about.

The Baron—a.k.a. Emperor Zarathustra I—bared his teeth to reveal two long fangs dripping venom like a snake's. His tentacles reached out from around his mouth and drew Nanni closer. He bit suddenly, deeply, and eagerly into her side. She convulsed three times and fell to the ground.

Dylan had to do something. But what could he do? A wall of Rolling Calves was headed toward him. There was still time for him to run and hide. The ground rumbled with the pounding of their hooves. The air was hot with their fiery breath. Flames ran up and down their long sharp horns and their eyes smoldered as they snorted ash and smoke. The wall of charging roaring burning snorting bull flesh and muscles and hooves was about to slam into him faster than a high-speed Internet connection.

Then it halted, as if an invisible barrier had come down between Dylan and the charging beasts.

The *Black Starr* had landed!

Dozens of pirates dressed in crimson and wielding swords charged off the ship and joined the battle against the Baron. There were pirate Rolling Calves, pirate Wata Mamas, pirate Maruunz, pirate Iron Lions—but far and away, most of the pirates were hummingbirds! The birds soared off the ship in a storm of swords, a frenzy of feathers, and a blaze of beaks. For a moment, the Baron's forces were thrown in disarray, startled by an attack by so many of the Baron's own people.

Dylan recognized one of the renegade birds.

"Don't look down," the patch-eyed hummingbird said as he flitted by, "on anyone." The ranking on the bird's chest was falling so fast Dylan couldn't even read the number.

Another pirate, a human one, swinging on a rope and holding a cutlass, set down right next to Dylan. She was tall, with her braided hair wrapped in a crimson-and-pink bandanna emblazoned with a skull and crossbones.

Emma? . . . It was Emma!

Dylan and his sister held each other for a good long while, heedless of swords and magic and charging beasts.

"I'm sorry for everything," Dylan began. "The portal, the Viral Emma video, the—"

"Break a vase," Emma interrupted.

"What?"

"*Break a vase—the love that puts it back together is stronger than the love that took it for granted when it was whole*. Derek Walcott said that."

"That's actually a good one," Dylan said. "Hey, what's with the birds? They're on our side?"

"A lot of the birds turned against the Baron," Emma explained. "They figured out that anyone who cares so much about money and power doesn't care about much else. You can't judge someone by their feathers! I got these recruits because of you!"

"How?"

"When I heard your Grand Chirp, I went to Ssithen Ssille. You were gone, but lots of birds wanted to sign up."

"So where is Ma Sinéad?"

Emma laughed. "You're looking at her!"

"You've got to be kidding me."

"There's a perfectly reasonable explanation . . ." But before Emma could finish, shards of glass flew through the air.

The Rolling Calves had knocked the *Black Starr* aside. They were on the move again—and the beasts had help. They were being led by a trumpeting Airavata—a nine-trunked elephant—and a Moongazer.

The Airavata was Anjali, one of the Loopy kids. It had to be. Even as a mythical beast she sounded like a French horn. And the Moongazer was that goon Chad who had chased Dylan out of school a million lifetimes ago. His gaseous body was still streaked with burns from Eli's fireblasts. Chad had bullied Anjali at school, now they were both among the many children hypnotized, bamboozled, and coerced into fighting the Baron's bloody battle. The Baron was baiting Dylan into an attack against people he knew. Here Anjali came, charging full force, her trunks in the air sounding death and destruction, her feet pounding out tremors as she approached ever closer. Chad, meanwhile, was rolling in like a fog bank. A Rolling Calf stampede was already unstoppable. This was beyond unstoppable.

Emma signaled to her pirate crew to take out the Airavata and the Moongazer.

"No!" Dylan yelled. "It's Anjali and Chad from school!"

"Really?"

"Anjali—wake up!" Dylan shouted at the rapidly approaching beast. "Chad—this isn't worth dying for!"

The Airavata plowed ahead. The Moongazer began roaring.

Emma placed a hand on her brother's shoulder. "Dylan—my crew will never stop them in time. We're both gonna get crushed! Nothing can stop a Rolling Calf stampede!"

Dylan had to clear his head and figure out what to do. Overstand. He remembered what he had in his pocket—a piece of that crimson feather.

"Take this," he told Emma. "It's not big enough for both of us."

She looked at him in wonder, and took the piece of crimson feather from his hand. She kissed Dylan on the cheek, then floated away. Dylan exhaled. Emma was safe now. But the Airavata, the Moongazer, and the Rolling Calves were a few stomps away. What was that saying? *Only death stops a Rolling Calf stampede.* Dylan knew what he had to do. He didn't have powers. He didn't have a cheat code. All he had was himself. He spread out his arms, closed his eyes—and braced for impact.

And that's when Dylan died.

CHAPTER THIRTY-TWO

And that's when Dylan was reborn.
He finally got his powers back.

Of course he had to die—it all made sense now! He was a duppy—a Caribbean ghost. The magic words that he'd seen written in the rock behind the waterfall when he first arrived in Xamaica blazed with complete clarity in his mind:

There is no way—but The Way
There is no time—but now

> *There is no love—but one love*
> *Anyplace, anytime, anyhow*
> *Give your life—and you will find it*
> *Lose your path—you won't be lost*
> *Don't waste time—for time's a-wasting*
> *Tomorrow begins today*
> *—The Inklings (H.G., J.K., C.S., J.R.R., E.G.)*

The Duppy Defender was back.

"It's on!" Dylan shouted.

He picked up the Airavata and carefully dropped her on a nearby hill. He knocked the Rolling Calves back like ants. And with a breath, he blew Chad away like so much smoke. He made sure none of them were hurt—and that they wouldn't be hurting anyone else.

He peered across the battlefield and fixed his gaze on his real target. The Crimson Beast had tried to destroy Dylan's family and friends. On this day, on this hour, at this defining moment, Dylan would take him on. Now he flew at the Baron. Actually took wing. All the abilities he had when he played the game of Xamaica returned to him now. He clawed at the Baron like an Iron Lion. He bound his limbs with webs like a giant spider. And finally he blew flame like a Rolling Calf and the Baron's feathers, so vulnerable to fire, crumbled into ashes.

His friends were at his side now, and Emma too, fighting against a sea of enemies. Eli snorted fire at the feathered dinosaurs and butted them with his flaming horns. Ines batted back attackers with swipes of her paws. Emma hacked and parried and sliced with her cutlass.

But the Baron had a final spell. As the tentacles around his beak waved and twisted, he began a guttural chant. The words were an ancient tongue, older than stone and sea. The children couldn't recognize the language but the meaning could be felt in their bones: it was a spell about greed. The desire for wealth, for power, for status—it was channeled into the Baron's obeah like a garbage chute. And the great Green Cloud that the Baron and his minions had stolen from the shadows and memories of Xamaicans was swiftly sucked and slurped into the gluttony.

Now a slimy green bubble was growing around the Baron, slick and bending the light like a smear of grease on a window. An awful wail went up from the battlefield, and the members of Nanni's forces dropped their weapons and grabbed their heads in pain and despair. Feelings of piggishness seemed to overwhelm all thought, avarice overcame every recollection, and greed, huge and insatiable, filled every heart. Some of the fighters fell to the ground, wiggling, their limbs melting away, their features fading.

"They're becoming worms!" Eli yelled.

Ines stuck out her tongue. "Gross! Why does it have to be worms? Why not fish? Don't birds eat fish? Or how about mice?"

A great depression seemed to sink every spirit. And still the bubble grew, bigger than the battlefield, expanding until it filled the sky, and all of Xamaica was under an ugly green light, the color of snot, an infected wound, or paper money.

Dylan's powers were starting to dissipate. His fireballs fizzled and his strength faded. A sweep of the Baron's tail knocked him to the ground.

"Dylan—what's the matter?" Ines asked.

"He can only copy the abilities of others for short bursts," Eli said. "He's becoming a regular dude again."

Newly powered by the bubble, the Baron melted the webs that held him and pinned Dylan to the earth with a taloned foot. His guards quickly subdued Ines, Eli, and Emma.

The Baron loomed over Dylan like a mountain. His tentacles twisted around his beak. His fangs were bared in a kind of awful smile.

At last—the Duppy Defender meets his fate! Now, I will feed on you as I feast on the worms!

But there was another game afoot.

It turned out Nestuh was one of those spiders who was good at *untying* things.

While the Baron reveled in his seeming victory, Nestuh had freed his remaining arms, wriggled away—and now stood alone beside the Great Drum of Anancy.

He beat the drum once and every creature halted, including the Baron. With that strike, barriers were broken and illusions were shattered. Creatures on the battlefield who imagined that the Baron's wooden carts carried the treasure of their fantasies, who thought that their vaults back home were laden with hummingbird-granted riches, were suddenly aware that, all along, they had been hoarding nothing but air.

Nestuh struck the drum eight times in all, and with each hit came a vision. Of a time when the creatures of Xamaica pulled together and not apart. When they worked to enrich the land, not just themselves. When they sought not simply for their wishes to be granted but struggled to make them come true. It was more than just a dream, it was a goal.

The Baron swept Dylan aside with a beat of his wings.

Get him! cried the Baron, pointing at the spider.

Nestuh tried to scamper away. But, mortally wounded and missing limbs, he didn't get far and never really had a chance. The Baron's guards easily pinned him down.

Finish him!

At that, his guards, using their knifelike claws, ripped Nestuh almost in two.

"Noooooo!" screamed Dylan.

The spider's body fell limp onto the battlefield. His remaining legs twitched once and then twice.

Then his body was still.

"Nestuh!"

Eli fought his way to where the great spider had fallen. He blazed a path through Higues and hummingbirds. Reaching the spot, he cradled Nestuh's head in his arms.

"Now I'm missing more legs than you." The spider smiled. "Can we be friends again?"

"We never stopped being friends!" Eli cried. "You're going to be okay! This isn't the end!"

The spider's eyes twinkled one last time. "Eli, my friend—have I taught you nothing about storytelling?"

And thus perished Nestuh Elisha of Akbeth Akbar, the 1,555th child in his family. Though he was one of many, he is the only member of his clan of whom the bards would sing.

Nestuh's beat, however, still echoed across the battlefield. It rattled the rocks and swayed the trees and shook the confidence of the members of all the armies. The dragons were suddenly doubtful. The Baron had lied about the wishcoins—so he couldn't be trusted about anything. The Iron Lions murmured in their ranks. Couldn't their differences be discussed? The hummingbirds were atwitter; leaving their weapons and armor behind, many of them flitted away to seek flowers to sip.

Above, in the middle of the sky, the bubble burst.

The Green Cloud split and the clean light of day swept across the battlefield. Sweet memories and precious recollections returned to their rightful owners. The Baron's plans had gone awry. And now, there was a sound, a Great Note, a Grand Chord, that reverberated across Xamaica— the final passage of a vast symphony.

"The sky is falling! The sky is falling!" Eli shouted.

The last strand had snapped, and the Great Web of the World was coming down.

The Baron's army scattered in fright. The web was an immense thing, wondrous in its design. Each strand was made up of many smaller stands, like a snowflake is made of smaller crystals. The strands of the web now separated, and, by some ancient obeah that went back to the time of the Great Weaving, the web fell on the Baron's army and not those who opposed them. It entangled Soucouyants and brought them down. It netted Higues and their burning eyes went out. It brought down flying dinosaurs that served as the Baron's personal guard.

The Baron himself reared up, caught in the sticky strands of the Great Web. He writhed and roared but could not free himself. The members of his army were in retreat, or captured, or had switched sides. Whatever hold he had on most of his followers had been broken by the beat of Nestuh's drum. The Baron was out of obeah and, with a final roar that blew away clouds and shook stone, he gave up his terrible gigantic form.

Emperor Zarathustra I was once again a hummingbird, a menace only to bugs and nectar. His number fell to 0. Everyone else's ranking blinked out.

Dylan flicked the Baron away with a finger.

After a day of terror, a mighty laugh rolled over the battlefield and the Baron fluttered into the forest and was not seen again in that form in this age of Xamaica. The Groundation had come to pass. The old world was over; a new one had been born.

In the distance, the Baron's tornado tower fizzled into a light breeze, and the roulette city went spinning off into the far distance. All bets were off.

Emma bounded onto the deck of the *Black Starr* and pointed her cutlass at the horizon, in the direction of the faraway nest trees.

"Alas for you who get evil gain from your houses, setting your nests on high, and believe yourselves to be free from ruin!" Emma cried. "The prophet Habakkuk."

"And *hasta la vista* too," Eli chimed in.

Dylan felt his body stiffen. He was becoming flesh and blood again—and he was having a seizure. There was a metallic taste on his tongue. He lost control of his arms and legs and fell to the earth. The world turned blurry and he felt like he was choking. With that, he saw and heard no more.

CHAPTER THIRTY-THREE

D ylan woke up beside a waterfall. He was resting on
soft grass and the flowers around him were singing.
There were two moons in the sky and he couldn't see the
Earth.

Ines, Eli, and Emma were standing over him.

"What happened?"

"You're back in your human form," Eli said. "Your avatar
is so powerful, there isn't enough magic to maintain it for
long."

"You also had a seizure," Emma said, "since video games

trigger them. So when you came here, it was only a matter of time before you had a big one. You need to rest."

"Where's the Baron?"

"His rule is over," Ines said.

Eli smiled. "All he left behind were a couple giant crimson feathers."

"So the web has fallen?" Dylan asked.

"Folks are just going to have to live up to the principles without it," Ines said. "Maybe it's better that way."

"How did you get here anyway?" Dylan asked Emma.

"I played Xamaica when you weren't around. I went way past the forty-fourth level, found this magic boat, and put together my own crew. I used a fake name, so I couldn't take my slot as a Game Changer."

"Ariel November? The girl picked before me? Why didn't you say something before?"

"Hello? Half the school still calls me Viral Emma! You think I needed one more thing to make me seem pirate crazy? Anyway, I became something of a legend around here. When the water flooded into the Mee Mansion, it took me by surprise—I had never entered Xamaica for real before, only as an avatar. The Baron ambushed me and my crew and I had to go into hiding. I sent my ship to get you when you first arrived, but the Baron destroyed it. It's a magic ship, though, so it wasn't wrecked for long. It took me all this time to get a new crew together and track you down."

"What happened to the real Ma Sinéad?"

"I don't know. Maybe every few years they have to change the person in the position. Like they do with popes, or poet laureates, or the guys who play James Bond."

"Well, I'm glad you're back!" Dylan exclaimed. "So where's Nanni? Is the witch okay?"

Eli and Ines looked at each other.

"Tell me," Dylan demanded, his voice tight with concern.

"You better go see her," Ines said softly.

Dylan went alone into a nearby grove of palm trees. Nanni was on the ground leaning her head against a trunk. It was the same tree into which Dylan had carved his name a lifetime ago.

She was holding her iron book close to her chest. He gently took it from her arms and knelt down beside her. "You knew the Baron would lose. The prophecy—the Baron's final victory would be your final defeat. It had a dual meaning. Once you lost, he couldn't win again. It was his final victory. The Baron was so bent on destroying you, he couldn't see that."

Nanni coughed, and blood stained her lips.

"You're not well," Dylan whispered. "What can I do?"

She stared at him, and pursed her lips a bit as if to say *shhhh*. Then she told him something he had sensed from the start, but didn't dare to hope.

(On Earth my name was Lunnette. His name was Griffith)

Lunnette and Griffith married and had a son. She cooked jerk pork in the kitchen, played chess in the living room, and sipped mango juice on the porch as she reflected on the treasures in her secret book. The days passed and she saw herself aging, as any human would. She could have lived forever in Xamaica. She gave up obeah for life on Earth.

But then came her mistake. No, she wouldn't call it

that, because she did what she had to do, what any mother would do. How would any parent feel, seeing their firstborn convulsed in seizures, his eyes rolling back in his head, his tiny mouth an oval of pain? The doctors told her then that there was no cure, that the condition was fatal, that the only only hope for her baby Dylan was a miracle.

So, without telling Griffith, Lunnette breeched the portal between worlds. She knew she was risking everything by doing so. She reached back to Xamaica to draw on her obeah, to cast a spell that would stop the seizures and save the life of her child, uttering the ancient words inscribed in stone by the Inklings themselves:

There is no way—but The Way
There is no time—but now
There is no love—but one love . . .

The spells did their work. Now, unless her baby came into contact with sorcery, he would be forever free from his ailment. Her spells also ensured that her new daughter, Emma, would be born without the magical malady.

But the Baron was watching. And when she cast her spell, it drew his eye. He knew he had at last tracked down his prey. It was then that he sent his spies to destroy her happiness. He dispatched a flock of hummingbirds to clog the engines of Griffith's aircraft. And the Baron himself arrived in the form of a feathered crimson beast to attack the plane. Without her spells, Nanni was unable to stop him—but she somehow survived the onslaught. Confused by the attack and shattered with grief, however, she thought she had lost a husband, a son, and a daughter. She returned to Xamaica, her power sapped for a time, and wandered the land. That was when she found The Way.

Emma was here now, kneeling beside Dylan. With eyes full of tears, Nanni peered at them both.

"Why didn't you tell me who you were when I first saw you in Xamaica?" Dylan asked.

(I couldn't let myself hope that it was true. Then, before the battle, I saw myself in your mind. And soon it all came back—a trickle, and then a flood. My time on Earth was like a different life. It was a sweet time. Perhaps in a way I made myself forget. I've now pieced together my memories, and I can picture what happened and how we were saved. On the plane, when we were crashing, your father gave his life tearing magic feathers from the Baron's chest that softened my landing and saved my life. I escaped back to Xamaica uncertain of where I had been and what exactly had happened. I thought you had perished—but now I know your father's actions saved both you and Emma)

She closed her eyes.

"My soul is satisfied. I am Nanni and Lunnette. I am warrior and mother." Her voice sounded thin and tired and happy. "And now I've found you—my children."

With those words, she put a single heart-shaped piece in the puzzle in Dylan's mind, and his family portrait was suddenly complete. He knew who he was.

Nanni spoke no more. Her cheek brushed against Dylan and, all at once, he had a flood of memories of cozy evenings and lazy afternoons, before he could walk or talk but not before he could feel love, when she was his mother and he was her child, and nothing in the whole world, or any other planet, really mattered but that tender fact.

Then her cheek grew cold, like a marble bust, and that was that. A flight of shadows came and bore Nanni away into the comforting darkness of the woods.

Some would tell the tale that moments later, on the place where Nanni's body rested, a great dandelion bloomed, went to seed, and sent offspring flying to all corners of Xamaica, where they flower still.

Dylan didn't cry but Emma did. So he held her until her tears stopped flowing. And for the first time he noticed how much his little sister looked like their mom.

They laid Nestuh to rest in the morning.

His people came from Akbeth Akbar and took his body back to that region in the south of Xamaica, where the great spiders live. There, they prepared for his passing in the traditional manner, holding a vast Weaving. Dylan, Ines, and Eli went with them, and were given the honor of carrying Nestuh's burial cocoon.

"If I hadn't left him to go after Nanni's book, he would still be alive," Eli sobbed. "I don't think I can ever forgive myself for that."

Ines turned to face Eli, and hugged him with her Iron Lion paws. "You don't have to forgive yourself," she whispered. "I'm doing it for you."

All 1,554 of Nestuh's siblings attended the Weaving, except a sister who was in the midst of delivering 2,765 babies of her own. The relatives gathered on a green hillside of a white cliff overlooking the harbor of Akbin Agneth. There, in the long grass, the spider sisters did their spinning, until they had woven a web larger than a ship's sail. One spider—bigger and grayer than the rest—stood near the top of the slope. She gave a welcoming wave to the hummingbirds watching the ceremony from the treetops. There was no trace of bitterness in her eight eyes.

"I am Kaysee, mother of Nestuh," she said in a voice smooth as silk. "We spiders believe that in Time Out of Mind, Anancy connected every living thing with a web. Because the web could not be seen, other creatures didn't believe it was real."

A breeze—flower-sweet, like the breath of Jah—caught the vast funeral web, which had been fastened with long strands, like a parachute, to the burial cocoon.

Nestuh's mother continued: "Anancy told the creatures of Xamaica, *When we pass from this world, we live our lives inside out. If you have sown hate, you will reap it. If you have loved, you will be loved. Truly, I say, you will find yourself in a web that you yourself have spun.* Will you be as content as Nestuh in the heaven that you create?"

The gust took the cocoon off the cliff, over the water, twisting into the sky. Thus Nestuh, the spider who couldn't weave a web, was borne spinning, at last, into the afterlife.

CHAPTER THIRTY-FOUR

The kids had lost Nanni and Nestuh; Ines, despite a long search, found no traces of her dad. This all took some getting over. In fact, they were things you could never really get over. Xamaica was rebuilding after the fall of the Baron. The Golden Grove had collapsed, and the trees and their golden bark had turned to dust. The Green Cloud was gone, replaced by blue sky. The hummingbirds were constructing nests closer to the ground now, and getting jobs that required a little less gambling and a lot more talent. Dylan, his sister, and his friends lingered in Xamaica—Ines spent most of her time searching for traces of her father—but after months passed, and the time felt right, they decided to depart.

"I never thought I'd say it, but I'm feeling a little homesick," Dylan confessed. "I miss the Professor. I even miss her birdcalls."

"I know the feeling," Eli agreed. "I'm dying for some *carne asada*."

Dylan tucked Nanni's book under his arm. "Are you guys sure? We only have one trip left."

Ines and Eli answered together: "Let's do this."

And so Hope Road appeared one last time and took the children where they needed to go.

The children materialized in the game room in the Mee Mansion. They poured out of the portal and splashed onto the floor of the chamber, perfectly dry.

The black tablet, which had been door-sized, now shrank to the size of a book again. A single crack ran down it. Nobody would be crossing into Xamaica that way again.

The kids looked like their old selves. Eli was in his chair, Ines had her long glossy locks, Emma had her pirate doll back, and Dylan was Dylan. In terms of Earth-time, they had only been gone for one night. No doubt there were all sorts of folks looking for them.

Dylan noticed that Emma still had her cutlass. "You never know," she shrugged.

Tears suddenly sprang into Ines's dark eyes and she turned her face away.

"What's the matter?" Eli asked.

Ines tried to choke back sobs. "I'm just thinking about my dad—"

An odd melody floated into the room. Someone was playing the piano.

Dylan cupped a hand to his ear. "That's the tune that unlocked the game."

Ines's eyes opened wide. "The one my father used to hum!"

It was hard to tell where it was coming from. The Mee Mansion was a big place and the sound seemed to echo through every wall. The melody that they had played to launch the game was only a few notes. Whoever was playing now had turned it into something grander. The music was alternately melancholy and exuberant, moving along in gentle passages before bursting into celebrations of sound that seemed to shake the floors, rattle the walls, and jangle the ceiling.

"It's coming from the piano room!" Eli said.

The kids were running now, and Eli was rolling as fast as he could. Ines made it there first and promptly screamed, "Dad?"

Dr. Mee was sitting at a piano in a room full of pianos. The other instruments had all been rigged to play what he was playing, and so the room, the whole mansion, was filled with music. Now a hundred pianos stopped playing all at once. Dr. Mee looked up from the keyboard and smiled. He stood up, raised his goggles, and adjusted his lab coat. Ines ran to him and they embraced for a long time as the echoes of the pianos gradually faded away into the far-off corners of the house.

"My little warrior," Dr. Mee said, brushing back a lock of Ines's hair. "That was the last song your mother ever wrote. How curious that it should bring you back to me!"

"I thought you were gone!" Ines cried.

"Part of me *is* gone. I can never go back to Xamaica—my shadow is destroyed, and without it my body would wither."

Indeed, Dr. Mee wasn't casting a shadow.

"I thought nobody could survive without a shadow," Ines said.

"Only one thing could save me and you found it."

"The Root of Xamaica?" Eli asked.

"Nanni said she was the Root," Dylan said.

"And she was right."

"I don't get it," Ines said.

"Nanni believed in herself," Dr. Mee explained. "It was the source of her strength. But we can all be the Root. Belief is the Root of everything. Because you believed in me and kept searching for me even though my shadow was lost, I was able to return."

"*As the shadow follows the body, as we think, so we become,*" Emma said. "Buddha said that."

Dr. Mee hugged Ines again. "It's time for me to show a little faith in you," he said. "I'm stepping down from my position as chairman and CEO of Mee Corp. The company will be liquidated, and the assets, along with all my wealth, will be used to compensate shareholders and help our former employees find new jobs." He turned to Eli. "Young man, I couldn't be sorrier about my conflict with your father. The Baron tricked us both into thinking we were the rightful originators of the Xamaica software."

"Thanks for saying that," Eli replied, "but corporate America still sucks."

CHAPTER THIRTY-FOUR

"Business can be dirty," Dr. Mee admitted. "That's why I'm leaving it behind."

"But what will you do?" Ines asked.

"What *won't* I do? You gave me a second chance. There's enough junk in this old mansion to fund my retirement. I want us to spend the next few years together. You're my greatest invention! You're going to get pretty sick of me."

"What about Xamaica? What about the game?"

"What about it? The real Xamaica will go on. But the game is finished." Dr. Mee said that the company had been bombarded with messages and calls from players in the last few hours. Xamaica had changed. There were no barriers—and no conflicts either. After the battle, avatars had suddenly found themselves free to roam the whole island—and were welcomed by the inhabitants. It was now an adventure game without much adventure.

"I'm glad the battle had an impact on the game," Dylan said, "but I don't think you have to cancel Xamaica. It's probably an even cooler game now. Keeping the peace is way more challenging than war."

Dr. Mee laughed. "Well, we shall see. We shall see." With that, he sat back down at the piano and resumed playing.

CHAPTER THIRTY-FIVE

It was time for the others to go home. Ines called her limo and they all got in.

"So, do you want it?" Dylan asked.

"What?" Eli replied.

"Nanni's book. The wealth of the world. You still haven't looked inside."

"When the book was virtual, I thought it was a treasure. Now that it's real, it's virtually worthless. Who would believe me? You keep it. It should stay in your family."

"No, I want you to have it."

Eli took the book from Dylan. He looked at it closely. Its cover was made of steel, not silver. And its pages were just ordinary animal hide, not gold leaf or some precious material. Eli rubbed its spine and opened it up. Then he laughed.

"What does it say?" Ines asked.

"*All the wealth of the world . . .*" Eli giggled.

"What?" Dylan asked.

"I guess I should be outraged or something," Eli sighed. "But I'm weirdly okay with this."

"Cut the suspense," Dylan blurted out. "Tell us what's in the book! Jewels? Spells?"

"Gold leaf? Stock certificates?" Ines added.

"The book is blank," Eli shrugged.

"Are you kidding me?" Ines exclaimed. "But we know Nanni wrote in that book!"

"That must be its magic—it's blank for each new owner," Dylan reasoned.

"Give it a tap," Ines suggested. "I'm always finding checks hidden in my birthday gifts. If it's under a mil, it'll still make a good bookmark."

"No—it's all good, I get it," Eli explained. "I don't need to look to hummingbirds or wishcoins or magic books for riches. I think this means I have to write my own story."

Eli pulled out a pen and wrote in the book:

If wealth is all you seek, you will never find what you're really looking for.

When they got to his stop, Ines, Emma, and Dylan helped him get his wheelchair to the doorway of his apartment.

"So I guess this is goodbye," Eli said.

"You're not getting rid of me that easy," Ines countered.

"What do you mean?"

"Why not work with me?"

"I thought Mee Corp. was bust. And my disgust for corporations hasn't changed in the last thirty minutes."

"We can start a new company. Your dad knows about start-ups—he can help. I have my own bank account. It should be enough to get things off the ground. I had this idea. Remember my global friends? We could launch a nonprofit foundation to help kids around the world. There's something there, right?"

"So it would be totally noncommercial? No pop-ups, no billboards, and no sky-writing?"

Ines nodded.

"Well, in that case, let's fast forward past me playing hard-to-get. When do I start?"

Ines smiled.

"Later, everyone." Eli waved and began to wheel away.

"*Buenas noches,*" Emma called out after him. "And I know you were the one who planted a virus in that *Pirate Girl* video to get everyone to stop watching!"

Eli turned and winked. "*Buenas noches,* Viral Emma." He rolled up the short walk to his house.

Next, the limo headed to Dylan and Emma's house.

"Do you two want some private time?" Emma asked, grinning, before stepping out and running to the door, leaving Dylan and Ines alone.

Ines coughed and hacked up a wad of fuzz. "Hairball. I must still have a little Iron Lion in me."

Dylan laughed. "I guess this is goodbye."

"Maybe, maybe not."

Dylan gave her a puzzled look.

"Did you ever think that maybe we have things turned around? Maybe Xamaica is the real world, and this is the game. Maybe that's what life is about. If we do better here, become better people, we'll move up a few levels—and we can go back."

Dylan hugged Ines in response, then got out of the limo and waved as it drove away.

Right at that moment, a trumpet blast echoed down the street. Only it was no brass instrument and it brought with it a stinky smell.

He turned around only to face Chad and five of his goons right there in front of him.

"Been waiting for you for hours, Loopy," growled Chad, who was holding Dylan's black, gold, and green skateboard. "This time you can't use your board to get away. I've been eating beans. Black beans, white beans, fava beans. Get ready for the gas."

"What do you want?"

Chad's eyes took on a haunted look. "I had this dream— this nightmare. You were in it. All of us were. Like we were in this big battle in Xamaica. All of us can remember it. Isn't that weird—all of us remembering the same dream?"

"Yeah, that's weird all right."

Chad got right in Dylan's face. Dylan could smell his too-familiar bubblegum breath. "You think it's easy coming to a new school?" Chad whispered. "I have to fight, man. It's kill or be killed."

"It doesn't have to be like this," Dylan said. "We're all birds of a feather. There's another way."

Chad's green eyes looked desperate—and then they turned mean again. He slammed Dylan's skateboard into a parked vehicle—which just happened to be the Professor's electric car. The board didn't break, but a side window did.

"So what I was saying before—was it a game or a dream or what?" Chad tugged one of Dylan's dreadlocks like he was trying to turn on a desk lamp. "Answer me, Loopy."

Dylan shifted into the first position of Bangaran, the backward hummingbird. Chad, startled by his move, stumbled backward and fell, letting the skateboard flip into the air. Dylan did a somersault and landed on the skateboard as it hit the ground. He could feel his Duppy Defender abilities flowing through his body. He hadn't left all his powers in Xamaica after all!

Chad leapt to his feet. "I am gonna end you!" He and his goons charged like bulls.

Dylan began to roll toward them, faster and faster, and just as they were about to collide, he steered his skateboard up above their heads.

The goons grabbed air. "H-h-how are you doing this?" Chad stammered.

Dylan flew off into the night sky, beyond the streets of New Rock, above the roofs of houses, over electric lines and treetops.

"Go ahead—run away!" Chad yelled after him. "You're no hero!"

Dylan smiled. Riding the night winds, he turned his skateboard around and sped up. Now he was flying at the goons full throttle from the air.

Chad and his buddies began to run in the other direction. Dylan landed behind them, picked up his skateboard, and watched them retreat into the night.

What was that quote Emma said? *Winning without fighting is the ultimate martial art.*

"Game over," Dylan whispered.

He headed up the walk to his apartment building. Emma had her pirate cutlass brandished as two other goons scampered away from her. She seemed taller, brighter, and bolder than ever. She pointed across the street at the Professor's electric car and the crack in the window vanished.

Emma grinned. "I guess some of the *Black Starr* rubbed off on me."

"I can see that," Dylan laughed.

"So are we gonna get along better from now on?"

"Depends. Are you gonna go pirate on me?"

Emma sheathed her cutlass. "I might."

"It's funny—before all this happened, I wanted to know about Mom and Dad so I could feel like I had a real family."

"And how do you feel now?"

Dylan smiled. "I miss Mom and Dad. But we've always had a family."

They opened the front door of their home together. Strange. It was late but all the lights were blazing. Inside, the Professor was sitting in the kitchen. All around her, her birds were quacking, cawing, cuckooing, hooting, tweeting, gobble-gobbling, cock-a-doodle-dooing, and all the other

275

things that feathered things do and a few things they don't, or at least they shouldn't. The Professor was weeping.

"It's my fault," she cried to herself. "I knew you were in danger. I knew something was after you. That something supernatural was afoot. I tried to watch the birds. I tried to protect you. I failed . . . I failed . . ."

Dylan thought of all the sacrifices the Professor had made, and the secrets she had kept—all for him. She needed some cheering up.

Dylan went up to her and put a hand on her shoulder. Emma took one of the Professor's hands in hers and smiled.

The Professor sat up in shock. "Where have you been?"

"Out," Dylan said. "But I think we're all going to stay here awhile."

He took out something he had brought back from Xamaica. Evidence of where they had gone, and the proof she needed to get her job back. He laid on the table a handful of giant crimson feathers.

The Professor smiled through her tears and held up a half-full glass. "Lemonade anyone?"

Outside, three little birds peeked in the kitchen window.

The End

GLOSSARY

Xamaicapedia:
The Gamer's Guide to Saving the World
A publication of Fiercely Independent Booksellers Inc.
(A wholly owned subsidiary of Mee Corp. Enterprises.)

During my research into Xamaica, I've noted many parallels with real-life Caribbean history and myth. While my *Xamaicapedia* goes into exhaustive detail on much of what I found, I thought an excerpt—a brief glossary of terms—might be helpful to some readers. The entries that had parallels in history or real-life folktales, I've marked with an **(R)**. I've also compiled a reading list that I think may help future explorers of this fascinating, dangerous, magical land.

—*E.G.*

Airavata (R): A white elephant with four tusks and seven trunks, from Hindu tradition.

Akbeth Akbar: The land ruled by the society of spiders.

Anancy (R): The trickster spider of Jamaican folk tales. The character—who has a lot in common with Br'er Rabbit, Bugs Bunny, and Spider-Man—has roots in African myth.

Arrowaks: In Xamaica, these are gentle plant people. *Arawak* was the name given to some of the original Indian inhabitants of the Caribbean region, many of whom were wiped out by European colonizers starting in the fifteenth century.

Babylon (R): The name Rastafarians give to the corrupt outside world; in Xamaica it's what they call *Earth*.

Bangaran (R): Kind of like karate with a Jamaican twist.

Baron Zonip: The ruler of the hummingbird kingdom and much of Xamaica.

Black Starr (R): Marcus Garvey (1887–1940) was a Jamaican-born political leader who later moved to America. He helped build a shipping fleet called the Black Star Line to transport passengers and goods and empower people of African heritage. In Xamaica, the Black Starr is an invisible ship that sails on the wind.

Crimson Vision: When Maruunz warriors come of age, their eyes turn red, their powers increase, and they get to take a real name.

Dead Yard (R): A funeral tradition where relatives and friends gather at the home of a recently passed loved one to share stories and memories. In Xamaica, it's the name given to the wasteland created after the Baron stripped the countryside of magic.

Dlos (R): Part-snake, part-human, mostly trouble. These have parallels in African legends.

Duppy (R): A kind of Jamaican ghost. My grandmother used to tell me, "Egbert"—that's my real first name—"if you don't behave the duppy is going to get you!"

Fist of Back-o-Wall (R): Back-o-Wall was a neighborhood of extremely poor people in Jamaica that was bulldozed by the government in 1965, displacing many residents against their will. In Xamaica, this magical glove helps bust through walls.

Game Changers: Are you one?

Golden Grove: A grouping of mahoe trees with silver trunks, platinum branches, and golden leaves where the richest hummingbirds live. The ultimate upscale address.

Great Web of the World: A vast weaving spun across the sky by the spider-god Anancy and held at the four corners of the world by Liberty, Equality, Vitality, and Mystery. But don't look to the sky for justice. Be fair and kind to everyone while your feet are on the ground.

Green Cloud: An information cloud milked from memories.

Groundation (R): It's a real term in the Rastafarian religion for a gathering, but in Xamaican mythology it's kind of like Ragnarok, Götterdämmerung, or the Apocalypse.

Hai-Uri (R): Found in African myth, this is a one-sided creature with a single eye, a single leg, and one hungry mouth.

Higue (R): Folks tell stories about these things in Guyana. In Xamaica, they're giant mosquitolike creatures that feast on blood. Imagine a tropical vampire and you're pretty much there.

Inklings (R): J.R.R. Tolkien (author of *The Hobbit*) and C.S. Lewis (author of *The Chronicles of Narnia*) were close friends, and formed a writers group in England. A group with the same name has cosmic significance among Xamaicans. I've been working hard to reach out to them, if they exist.

Iron Lions: Half-man, half-lion, these beasts have metal wings and speak in questions. There's a Bob Marley song called "Iron Lion Zion."

Jah (R): The name for God in the Rastafarian religion.

Machete of the Land of Look Behind: A blade forged by Queen Nanni that bursts into flame when there is bravery in the wielder's heart.

Ma Sinéad: Xamaica's own pirate queen. Some real-life women joined pirate crews in the Caribbean, notably Anne Bonny and Mary Read in the eighteenth century.

Mee Corp.: The world's largest manufacturer of electronic dreams.

Luscas (R): Part-shark and part-squid; there are stories about these creatures around the Caribbean. In Xamaica, they are also part-vulture.

Maruunz (R): When the British took over Jamaica from the Spanish in 1655, many African slaves fled into the interior of the island and set up free communities. Employing complex guerrilla tactics, these people—who came to be known as Maroon warriors—successfully fought the better-armed British for hundreds of years and forced the invaders to sign a peace treaty in the eighteenth century. In Xamaica, the Maruunz are great warriors.

Moongazers (R): These bearlike creatures sport savage claws and bodies of mist. They are among the most fearsome creatures in Xamaica. Guyanese legends tell similar tales.

Nanni (R): Queen Nanny (c. 1685–c. 1755), along with the rebel Cudjoe, led the Maroons in their resistance against the British. The Jamaican government declared Nanny a national hero in 1976 and her portrait appears on the country's $500 bill. Legend says she had magical powers. As for Nanni, I see her dark eyes in my dreams.

Nestuh (R): Nesta Robert Marley is the birth name of Bob Marley (1945–1981), the musician who helped make Jamaican reggae music famous around the world.

Obeah (R): The Jamaican—and Xamaican—word for magic.

Palm of Protection: A magic tree whose seeds have spread. Nothing may harm you while you rest among its fronds, and nothing can find you unless you want to be found.

Rolling Calf (R): Half-man, half-bull, all on fire. Jamaicans tell stories about Rolling Calves.

Shatranj (R): A board game of strategy and mental focus that's a lot like chess.

Si-Ling: The empire of the Rolling Calves.

Soucouyant (R): Human by day, by night this creature slips out of its skin and becomes a fireball-throwing, flesh-eating plant. A remix of a Caribbean myth.

Ssithen Ssille: The hummingbird kingdom.

Steel Donkey (R): Just what it sounds like.

Time Out of Mind: What Xamaicans call the olden days, when Jah walked the earth and Anancy spun webs in the sky.

Toljabee (R): A Korean celebration during which a baby picks up various items spread out on a table that are said to predict the child's future. Yongjin, this book's illustrator, never told me what he selected, but maybe someday I'll ask.

Wata Mama (R): A playful water creature with a seal-like body from African myth. They're cute and all, but terrible fighters.

The Way: It's all around you.

Wholandra: The city of the Iron Lions.

Wishcoins: Currency established in Xamaica during the Baron's rule. Wishcoins, which cannot be seen or touched, can be redeemed for wishes from the Iron Lions. But you're better off going to school and getting a job.

Zion: What do you believe?

RECOMMENDED READING

Tales of Old Jamaica and *History of Jamaica*, by Clinton V. Black

Before the Legend: The Rise of Bob Marley, by Christopher John Farley

The Mother of Us All: A History of Queen Nanny, by Karla Lewis Gottlieb

Kingston: A Cultural and Literary Companion (Cities of the Imagination), by David Howard

Life Among the Pirates: The Romance and the Reality, by David Cordingly

The Boy from Nine Miles: The Early Life of Bob Marley, by Cedella Marley and Gerald Hausman

Selected Poems, by Claude McKay

The Story of the Jamaican People, by Philip Sherlock and Hazel Bennett

The Heinemann Book of Caribbean Poetry, featuring Derek Walcott and others

C.J. FARLEY was born in Kingston, Jamaica, and grew up in Brockport, New York, with stops in Middle-Earth, Earthsea, and Narnia. Farley's biography Aaliyah: More Than a Woman *was a national best seller. A former editor of the* Harvard Lampoon *and a former music critic for* Time, *Farley is a blogger, columnist, and senior editor at the* Wall Street Journal. Game World *is his first novel for young readers.*

YONGJIN IM is an illustrator by night and a corporate lawyer at all other times of the day. Born in Seoul, Korea, but raised in Maryland, Im is a former art director for the Harvard Lampoon. Game World *is the first book to feature his artwork and the drawings of his daughters, Allegra and Ines.*

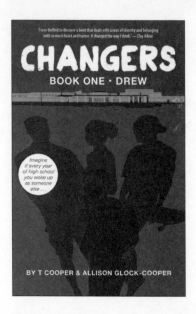